Charles H. Levermore

The Town and City Government of New Haven

Charles H. Levermore

The Town and City Government of New Haven

ISBN/EAN: 9783337406240

Printed in Europe, USA, Canada, Australia, Japan

Cover: Foto ©Andreas Hilbeck / pixelio.de

More available books at **www.hansebooks.com**

THE TOWN AND CITY GOVERNMENT OF
NEW HAVEN

JOHNS HOPKINS UNIVERSITY STUDIES

IN

HISTORICAL AND POLITICAL SCIENCE

HERBERT B. ADAMS, Editor

History is past Politics and Politics present History.—*Freeman*

FOURTH SERIES

X

THE TOWN AND CITY GOVERNMENT OF NEW HAVEN

By CHARLES H. LEVERMORE, Ph. D.

Fellow in History, 1884–5, Johns Hopkins University

BALTIMORE

N. MURRAY, PUBLICATION AGENT, JOHNS HOPKINS UNIVERSITY

October, 1886

ISAAC FRIEDENWALD, PRINTER,
BALTIMORE.

CONTENTS

THE TOWN AND CITY GOVERNMENT OF NEW HAVEN.

I.

THE DUAL GOVERNMENT. 1784–1886.

Town-Born vs. Interloper.

The incorporation of New Haven City, like most progressive measures, was achieved in the face of no little opposition. City privileges must have been deemed Grecian gifts in those days, for the dispute over the same subject in Hartford was still more animated and prolonged. The change in New Haven was wrought out through friction between several strongly-defined elements in society. The staid, conservative families and the younger, enterprising business men who together made the town, rallied in two camps, which were described in the local vernacular as " The Town-Born" and "The Interlopers." This odd division seems to date from the days when New Haven's commerce revived, perhaps about 1760. Those who had breathed the air of New Haven at their first entrance into this world, sometimes looked askance at the influx of bustling traders, shippers, and professional men not "to the manner born"; while those individuals whose ancestry had sat in Robert Newman's barn, and had worshipped from generation to generation in the First Church, perched aloft upon social summits that have not yet been entirely leveled. These people were grieved by the destruction of their quiet town-life, by the intrusion of a rabble of sailors and workmen, and, above all, by the insurgent spirit of unrest that came with the ships and strangers. The interlopers, on the other hand, were most directly responsible for the new commercial activities of the place. Among them were ambitious, aggressive, and broad-minded men, ready to promote progress in municipal as well as in personal affairs. The number of inhabitants in New Haven in 1748, the township including the half-dozen out-lying parishes, was about 1,400. The official records of Connecticut in 1756 attribute to New Haven a population of 5,085. An increase of 3,600 in eight years was, at that time, a very prosperous growth. In 1774, the inhabitants numbered 8,022. The average annual increment from 1724 to 1748 was 20; between 1748 and 1774 it was nearly 255. The augmentation of wealth during the latter period out-stripped that of the population. Compared with the former two decades, the amount of tonnage in the port had increased over forty-fold, and the value of exports had been multiplied by 470.

Such were the results of the re-infusion of the commercial spirit into the veins of Eaton's torpid town. However, it is not supposed that the business interests of the community were helplessly dependent upon sharp social distinctions. Not all the town-born eschewed business enterprise, neither did the life of the place spring wholly from young and imported blood. The feeling between town-born and interloper became an instinct, an inherited sentiment, powerful in politics and society, but often almost entirely dissociated from original conditions. Instances are not wanting of the outcropping of this old antipathy from beneath the deposits of years of social growth. Sometimes the interests of the town-born were very sternly sundered from those of the interloping element. Mr. Trowbridge relates that one Capt. Brown, being compelled by stress of storm to throw overboard some portion of his cargo, ordered that the goods of inter-lopers should be selected for the libation to Neptune, but that the consignments to town-born people should be saved.

Leaders of the interloping element before the Revolution were men like Benedict Arnold, Col. David Wooster, the

hero of Danbury, James Hillhouse, the most public-spirited
and generous of citizens; above all, Roger Sherman, the foremost man in New Haven, if not in the State, throughout one
generation.   It is safe to say that while he lived he was the
head and front of every species of good work for his adopted
home.   Sherman, Wooster, and Hillhouse were interested, in
1771, in the movement toward the formation of a city, and,
when the close of war afforded once more an opportunity for
domestic improvement, Roger Sherman was the central
figure around which the progressive elements in society
clustered.   Starting in life as an apprentice to a Massachusetts shoemaker, he became a member of the Connecticut
Council, a Judge of the Superior Court, a member of the
Revolutionary and Continental Congresses, wherein he
belonged to the committee that reported the Declaration of
Independence, a member of the United States Constitutional
Convention, a Representative and afterward a Senator in
Congress under the Constitution.   Among the prominent
leaders of that era, he enjoyed the rare honor of affixing his
signature to the four most important documentary expressions
of the new national unity, " The Address to the King,"
" The Declaration of Independence," " The Articles of Confederation," and " The Constitution."   Throughout the latter
part of his career he was dowered with "pluralities" like a
mediæval prelate.   At his death, in 1793, he was a United
States Senator, a Judge of the Superior Court of Connecticut,
and Mayor of the city of New Haven.   To that infant city,
indeed, he maintained a relation quite comparable to that
which subsisted between the ancient town and its Governor,
Theophilus Eaton.   Mr. Sherman's unsympathetic character,
however, could not command that universal allegiance which
waited upon the Puritan patriarch.

First Phases of City Politics.

The distinctions of Patriot and Tory intersected society and
envenomed the neighborhood animosities.   The town had

officially promised, as we have seen, to forgive and forget, but the diary of President Stiles shows how beneath the surface the poison rankled.[1] A combination of interlopers, business men, and Tories, the latter probably actuated by political motives mainly, was most actively interested in the fortunes of the new city. Out of about six hundred adult males then living within the city limits, the selectmen certified that 343 were qualified[2] to be freemen. About one-fourth of the latter number failed to take the oath, so that there were only 261 qualified citizens at the time of the first election, February 10, 1784. The poll for Mayor showed 249 votes, of which Roger Sherman received 125—just enough to elect him. Thomas Howell, deacon of the First Church, received 102 suffrages, while 22 freemen preferred Thomas Darling, who was probably the choice of the extreme Tories. Deacon Howell, who was, like Sherman, an inter-loper, was elected to be Senior Alderman. Three other Aldermen were named—viz.: Samuel Bishop, Deacon David Austin, and Isaac Beers, the bookseller. Provision was made, as the law required, for a City Clerk, two Sheriffs, a Treasurer, and for twenty Councilmen. About one hundred citizens completed the election of the latter on the third day (February 12), when the new officials were formally inducted into office. Inasmuch as the charter directed that the municipal year should begin in June, the forms of election were repeated on the following first of that month. On the day after the close of the February election, Dr. Stiles sketched a bird's-eye view of the political situation.

" The city-politics are founded in an endeavor silently to bring Tories into an equality and supremacy among the Whigs. The Episcopalians are all Tories but two, and all qualified on this occasion though despising Congress govern-

[1] See Prof. F. B. Dexter's excellent paper on New Haven in 1784.

[2] Suffrage was limited to those who held personal estate worth at least £40, or real estate renting for £2 per annum. Loyalty to Great Britain might also be a cause for disfranchisement.

ment before; they may, perhaps, be forty voters. There may
be twenty or thirty of Mr. Whittlesey's meeting added to
these.[1]   Perhaps one-third of the citizens may be hearty
Tories, one-third Whigs, and one-third indifferent.   Mixing
up all together, the election has come out, Mayor and two
Aldermen, Whigs; two Aldermen, Tories.   Of the Common
Council, five Whigs, five flexibles but in heart Whigs, eight
Tories; Sheriffs and Treasurer, Whigs, but one flexible."
Evidently the arrangement was not quite satisfactory to the
"inflexible" President of Yale.

THE FIRST CHARTER.

The Act of January 8, 1784, which was New Haven's first
city charter,[2] had incorporated the inhabitants of that portion
of the town of New Haven which lay between the Quinnipiac and West Rivers, and between the Mill River meadows
and the harbor, under the title, "The Mayor, Aldermen,
Common Council, and Freemen of the City of New Haven."
We have seen that twenty Councilmen were at first elected.
The number of Councilmen was, however, a fluctuating
quantity.   Twenty was fixed by the charter as the maximum
limit.   The list was soon reduced to ten, it was increased to
twelve, then to fourteen, and in 1853 the original membership was restored.   The city legislature comprised the Councilmen, the Aldermen and the Mayor.   Under the name of the
Court of Common Council, it was empowered in general
terms to regulate local affairs, to afford security to property
and person, and to provide for the convenience of trade.   The
city was not divided into wards, so that the legislative body
was not based upon a neighborhood constituency.   The
Aldermen were chosen, practically, as assistants to the Mayor,
and the chief functions of both Mayor and Aldermen were

---

[1] Mr. Whittlesey was pastor of the First Church.
[2] The text of the Act can be found in Conn. Private Acts, I. 406,
and in the City Year-Book for the years 1876-78.

judicial. In conformity with venerable English usage, the
City Court was the Mayor's court, wherein that official and
the two Senior Aldermen presided. The other two Aldermen
were Judges in reserve. The new City Court wielded a jurisdiction like that of the Court of Common Pleas in all civil
causes originating within the bounds of the city, except such
as concerned land-titles. At least one of the parties to a
suit must be a resident of the city. The criminal jurisdiction
of the court was confined to offenses against the city ordinances. Justices of the Peace for the town still dispensed the
ordinary criminal justice. The Mayor and his four Aldermen
bear a definite resemblance to the magistrate and deputies,
the Reeve and Four, with whom New Haven started in 1639.
The ancient institutional stock of the five elders clung
tenaciously to the New Haven soil.

Finally, all the freemen, in full City-Meeting assembled,
were the ultimate arbiters of all municipal questions. This
purely democratic assembly.alone could levy taxes, and elect
officers. Its ratification was absolutely essential to every
by-law enacted by the Mayor and Common Council. Even
then no by-law was valid until it had been published for three
weeks successively in "Some public newspaper, in or near
said city." This arrangement seems sufficiently clumsy, but
the most remarkable check yet remains. Any by-law of the
city might be repealed within six months after enactment by
any Superior Court holden in New Haven County, if the said
Superior Court judged the by-law to be unreasonable or
unjust.[1]

Such pains were taken to prevent arbitrary municipal rule;
yet in one instance the charter itself trod closely upon vested
privileges. The city was empowered to exchange or sell the

---

[1] The English "Municipal Corporations Act" of 1882 provides that an
order of a borough-council for the payment of money may be taken to the
High Court of Justice by writ of *certiorari*, and may there be wholly or
partly disallowed or confirmed, with or without costs, as pleases the
court.

northwestern portion of the Green, in order to secure other land or highways, or another Green. These clauses were intended to notify the Proprietors' Committee that its authority over the public square was henceforth vested in the city, and that the proprietors could no longer vote away building-sites upon the Green. However, the remainder of the Green was confirmed as a common or public walk, to remain so forever, never liable to be laid out in highways or to be appropriated to any other purpose.

Jealousy of corporate action and the assertion of State legislative supremacy were distinctive features of this early charter. Public sentiment in 1784 regarded a city as a hot-bed of aristocracy, and a single executive officer, whether local or national, as a possible Julius Cæsar. The successive obstacles to the full habilitation of a city ordinance, the rati-fication by the citizens, the three weeks' publication in a newspaper, and the possible veto by the Superior Court, would check in our day not only the centralization of power, but also the transaction of business. In 1784, "Thou shalt not go slowly" had not become an American eleventh com-mandment.

The State Legislature reserved to itself ample oversight in the affairs of the new municipality. The Mayor, although elected in the first instance by the people, held his office during the pleasure of the General Assembly—a reservation which tended to make him Mayor for life. This tenure of the Mayoralty endured until 1826—a period of forty-two years. During that time New Haven was ruled by four Mayors, two of whom died in office and three of whom enjoyed an aggregate term of thirty-eight years. During the forty-two years next ensuing after 1826, the city has elected eighteen different Mayors. Moreover, the election and tenure of Probate Judges were both subject, until 1851, to the Gen-eral Assembly. In the *personnel* of the town government the establishment of the city wrought no change, and the functions of town officers were altered, if at all, in amount, but not in kind.

DESCRIPTION OF THE CITY.

The city proper of New Haven, in 1784, was the small
nucleus of the town, and situated at the edge of the harbor;
but the city limits included Davenport's original town plat
and the two miles square, with the common fields and pas-
tures. Although General Garth, in 1779, had thought New
Haven too fine a place to burn, it was but a straggling
village of 3350 inhabitants. In its centre was the unfenced,
unkempt Green, marked by wagon-ruts and disfigured by
weeds and bushes. Against this unsightly growth, as well
as against the nomadic geese and swine, the village fathers
had long waged an unavailing paper warfare. In the southwestern corner of the Green, nearly opposite the New Haven
House of our day, stood the old County House and Jail,
removed in the spring of 1784, at an expense of £30, across
the street into what is now the College campus. Near them
the old State House, erected in 1717, was situated, and was
now perhaps used by the grammar school. The building
which had superseded it in 1763, "The New Brick State
House," formed with the First and the " Fair Haven " Congregational Churches a line of edifices upon Temple street.
The only other churches in the city were the " Blue Meeting-
house,"[1] or "White Haven Church," at the southeast corner
of Elm and Church streets, and the Trinity Episcopal, on
Church street. Two college-buildings, South Middle and
the Athenæum, held the Yale of that day, though the first
college-edifice was still standing, much dilapidated, in the
southeast corner of the campus. Doubtless the sight of a
college and a jail thus jostling each other caused more than
one jocular remark in the hamlet. Student-life was boisterous
then, and was destined to become more so.

---

[1] So called on account of the color of the paint used upon it.

MUNICIPAL IMPROVEMENTS.

A multitude of good works followed upon the new order of municipal duties. The first city tax of one penny in the pound was decreed.[1] The first by-law forbade the erection of buildings without a permit under a penalty of ten pounds, the heaviest fine which the Council was allowed to inflict. There was a flavor of antiquity in the agreement that meetings of the City Council should be called by " Posting notices on each corner of the eight central squares." In addition a bell was to be rung, and proclamation of the day and hour made, at each corner. By September this method of convocation was deemed inadequate, and the City Clerk was instructed to notify members of the government whenever the Mayor ordered a meeting. The tolling of the State House bell summoned the annual City-Meetings on the first Tuesday of every June at nine o'clock A. M.

As soon as the first municipal year was fairly begun, the Council labored vigorously at its work of construction. It was determined that New Haven's trade should be as honest as official supervision could make it. In July, by-laws were passed creating a large number of inspectors and gaugers.[2]

---

[1] Taxes upon the dollar were not laid until July, 1709, when the rate was fifteen mills.

[2] The City Government, during its first quarter century. Elected by the freemen of the city: The Mayor, tenure of office at pleasure of General Assembly; 4 Aldermen, term one year; Councilmen (not more than 20), term one year; Sheriff, City Clerk, Treasurer, Tax Collector, each, term one year; Gaugers of Molasses, Rum, and other Spirituous Liquors; Inspectors of Pot and Pearl Ash; Inspectors and Cutters of Hoops, Staves, Heading, and Ready-Made Casks; Inspectors and Cutters of Plank, Boards, Clapboards, Oars, Shingles, and Scantling; Weighers of Hay; Inspectors and Measurers of Wood; Inspectors of Wheat, Rye, Indian Corn, and Flour; Inspectors and Packers of Beef, Pork, and Fish; Pound-keepers; Inspector of Tobacco; 6 Fire Wardens (after 1788); Board of Health (after 1794).

Elected by the Court of Common Council: 144 Jurors of the City Court; City Attorney (after 1803).

Articles offered for sale must bear the stamp of official
approval. Even prices of board and lodging were fixed
by law. There were enactments against nuisances, against
obstruction of highways, and against disregard of sanitary
precautions. One of the earliest ordinances provided for the
establishment of a public market. The ordinance was from
time to time suspended until, in the next year, two city
markets were built by subscription, one on the southeast
corner of the Green, the other where the present city market
stands. All retailing of meat and vegetable products elsewhere, between sunrise and eleven o'clock of the forenoon, was
forbidden under penalty of twenty shillings. A long and
bitter controversy arose over the merits of a public market
as opposed to individual peddling, or the old-fashioned street-
market in wagons. The city was never contented with the
conclusion that had been reached, and, after much trouble
and ill-feeling, the market law was formally repealed in June,
1826. President Dwight, who was a zealous champion of
the city market, called its overthrow "A striking example of
the power of habitual prejudice."[1]

In June of the initial year the charter was found lacking
in an unexpected quarter. The little village-city felt unable
to extend a suitable welcome to distinguished aliens. So the
needful legislation was procured from the General Assembly,
and the "freedom of the city" was soon after bestowed
upon the "Hon. William Michael St. John de Crevecœur,
Consul-General to His Most Christian Majesty for the States
of Connecticut, New Jersey and New York"; also upon his
children and upon his wife, "Mehitabel." In the following
spring, the "freedom" of New Haven was again granted to
a handful of dukes and princelings. Among the company
were the Duc de la Rochefoucault, the Marquis de St. Lam-
bert, and M. de la Custelle, *avocat du parlement.* To welcome

---

[1] He says: "There is something very remarkable in the hostility of the
New England people to a regular market." (Travels, I. 195.)

and convey these honored and honorable strangers, all the
half-dozen carriages in the city must have been required.
Public vehicles were heavy responsibilities in those days, for
every professional carter was compelled not only to carry a
license, but also to give a surety of one hundred pounds.

The city was disposed to foster immigration, and an
elaborate welcome was prepared for visitors of a lower degree
than the French nobility. A City-Meeting, held September
23, 1784, appointed a Committee of Hospitality, consisting
of Charles Chauncey, Pierpont Edwards, James Hillhouse,
Timothy Jones, Jonathan Ingersoll, David Austin, and Isaac
Beers, Esqrs. Their duties were " To assist all such strangers as shall come to the city for the purpose of settlement
therein, in procuring houses and land on the most reasonable
terms, and to prevent such persons, so far as possible, from
being imposed upon with respect to rent and the value of
houses and lands, and to give them such information and
intelligence with respect to business, markets, commerce,
mode of living, customs and manners, as such strangers may
need; and to cultivate an easy acquaintance of such strangers with the citizens thereof, that their residence therein
may be rendered as agreeable and eligible as possible." If
this programme was carefully followed, the home-seeker must
have thought New Haven a true Arcadia. Yet working-
men of the better sort were not attracted, unless President
Dwight's opinion of his fellow-citizens was untrustworthy.
While he extolled the intelligence and virtue of the community in general, he branded the artisan and laboring classes,
both white and black, as abnormally vicious.

In the autumn of 1784, suitable names were ordered for
the various roads, ways, and alleys within the town-plot, and
the first year of urban existence closed with an application to
the General Assembly for wider powers, especially in
respect to the laying out of highways. In the next year the
State of Connecticut, in the exercise of its sovereign powers,

established a mint at New Haven, and issued coinage therefrom until 1787.[1]

Contrary to the usual custom, neither town nor city was inclined to waste words over the Constitution of 1787, probably because there were few malcontents. The town recorded its desire for a convention of ratification, and appointed Roger Sherman and Pierpont Edwards delegates. There was no other official reference to the momentous change from a confederation to a nation, but public sentiment, as voiced in the journals, was enthusiastic in its support of Federalist principles.

The town began to feel pricks of conscience about disposing of paupers at a yearly auction, and, in 1785–86, the Town-Meeting declared that " The Town's-poor should be kept by themselves at one place, unless some of those who now have them offer to keep them at a manifestly cheap rate." There were then thirty-seven paupers, costing £12 per week, exclusive of clothing and doctors' bills. Three years later, when it was temporarily the fashion to let out most of the town's yearly expenses by contract to some one individual, there were but £270 paid for the support of the poor.

Both town and city discussed the erection of a workhouse until 1791, when it was built. The Town-Meeting of June 25, 1792, adopted what it called " The Workhouse Byelaws," which had been prepared by a committee. Any assistant, or justice of the peace resident within the town, might send to the workhouse for not more than three months, " Rogues, vagabonds, sturdy beggars, lewd, idle, dissolute, profane and disorderly persons, all runaway stubborn Servants and children, Common Drunkards, Common Night-

---

[1] A Connecticut copper cent from this mint, found in the basement-wall of the Hartford City Hall, bore on the obverse side the head of the Governor (probably Gov. Huntington), with the words " Autori. Connec." On the reverse were a female figure holding an olive branch, and the inscription " Inde. et Lib., 1787."

walkers, Pilferers, all persons who neglect their callings, mis-
spend earnings and do not provide for their families, and all
persons under distraction unfit to be at large and not cared
for by their friends or relatives." Such a motley company
might be punished, if need were, by the master of the house,
upon the approval of his superiors, by "Fetters or Shakles,
by whipping on the naked body not more than ten stripes at
one time, or by close confinement without food and drink."
Upon release, the criminals might claim two-thirds of their
earnings, minus the cost of commitment and support.
Criminals, paupers, and lunatics continued to be thus
housed under one roof until the middle of the next century,
when the growing scandal shocked the better class of citizens
into action.

THE FIRE DEPARTMENT.

The fire department of the city made its humble beginning
in January, 1788, when a "Fire Engine" was ordered at the
expense of the city. Frequent legislation for three years finally
gave the control of the department to six Fire Wardens, under
whom the entire male population of the city between the ages
of 16 and 60 was enrolled. To begin with, there had béen but
two fire companies, of seventeen men each. Practice with the
engines in "Washing and Playing" was ordered on the first
Saturday of every April, July and October. Every one must
attend with bucket or pail under peril of a two-shilling fine.
Ministers, and the President, tutors, and students of Yale College were alone exempted. Moreover, the Fire Wardens were
empowered to appoint four sackmen, "Respectable free-
holders, each of whom on every alarm of fire shall take with
him to the said fire one or more sacks and shall take care of
all property necessary to be removed from danger of fire."
There was one clumsy check to the extensive power of a Fire
Warden: no building could be destroyed, in order to prevent
the spread of fire, until the consent of the Mayor, Aldermen,
and the body of Fire Wardens, or the major portion of them,

had been obtained. No part of the city organization was so frequently tinkered as the fire department. Rigid rules fettered the action of the householder in minute details, and heavy fines were imposed—on paper. The fines were also inflicted, generally to be remitted at the next City-Meeting. Not only the erection of a stove, but even of a stove-pipe, without the permission of the Fire Wardens, was strictly prohibited. Oddly enough, the city re-enacted almost the same laws that had been framed in the same town in 1640, forbidding the kindling of bonfires in the street, or the smoking of tobacco within four rods of a building, and also enjoining the stated cleaning of chimneys. But the anti-tobacco legislation could not be enforced, and all the regulations brought neither safety nor satisfaction until the modern day of steam and electricity.

Danger from fire was no more dreaded than danger from small-pox. That scourge visited the community, as it had done thirty years before, with the revival of commerce. Both town and city moved to erect a small-pox hospital. A strict quarantine was maintained against all comers from New York. The town voted that "Laḥen Smith, who has come into the harbor with passengers from New York who do not belong to this Town," might land them on the east side of the harbor, provided that "They make off in a stage, and do not endanger the Town."[1] When it was announced in Town-Meeting, August 29, 1794, that a vessel was coming up the harbor, Mr. Adee was sent at once to the waterside, commissioned by the meeting to prevent any boat from landing. At the same time three physicians were elected health officers for the port. The city followed suit in the ensuing spring with the establishment of the first Board of Health. The mind of the city was especially exercised about the East Creek, which had become a receptacle of filthy drainage. The Board of Health consisted of ten persons, under the style and title of "The Health Committee of the City of New

---

[1] Records, V. 247.

Haven." It had full power to abate nuisances, and to improve, as it saw fit, the sanitary condition of the city. Through the labors of this committee, the local authorities obtained from the Legislature power to establish a quarantine for foreign vessels. The community became both unhealthy and impoverished. Although the trade of the place grew rapidly, the city felt the weight of the financial pressure that was universal in the nation. It was very difficult to secure adequate taxation. As a sign of the times, the path to the Treasury was more and more securely hedged in. In 1790, the City Clerk was constituted the sole drawer upon the Treasury, and his orders must first be certified by the Mayor. At the same time it was provided that, so often as there was no cash in the Treasury, the Treasurer should number and register each bill that was presented, and should pay the same in the order of presentation. Both town and city were indebted, apparently, even for the running expenses, and every new street or turnpiked road might be the occasion of fresh borrowing. • In 1802, the town-tax was five cents on the dollar, and a committee, of which Noah Webster was a member, was alarmed by a debt of $3,000.

All the work of the Board of Health was performed at its own expense. Most of the public improvements of the time, in the way of adornment or of more efficient sanitation, were dependent upon private funds and private energy. One of the very first acts of the City Government, in February, 1784, was to vote that "Any gentlemen who might agree to defray the expense" could enclose the southeastern part of the Green so as to admit footmen only, "Sufficient room being allowed for carriages before the public buildings." In the same independent way roads were improved, streets opened, and meadows diked and drained.

ADORNMENT OF THE GREEN.

First and foremost in these enterprises were two public-spirited and wealthy citizens, David Austin and James

Hillhouse. To them principally were due the rescue of the Green from its primitive savagery, its enclosure within fences, and its adornment with trees. Not the least of the improvements was the institution in 1796 of the Grove Street Cemetery, which was then a sort of wonder of the world, and the abandonment of the old burying-ground in the rear of the Centre Church—an improvement first proposed by Governor Francis Newman, in 1659. Yet the acts by which the city granted permission for these labors concluded significantly, "Provided the same be done without expense to the city." There was active opposition to the whole procedure, not only within the city, but in neighboring towns. The rejection of the graveyard on the Green seemed to the more ignorant and conservative classes both expensive and sacrilegious, and it was urged against Mr. Hillhouse in a political canvass twenty years afterward.

However, there is evidence that, after the beautifying was completed, the city repented and made a small contribution. The gentlemen who had been most active in the reform were appointed as a sort of Park Commission, their chief anxieties being due to Yale students and to geese. Against the latter bipeds a ponderously-framed law was proclaimed: "No goose or gander shall be allowed to go at large within the limits of New Haven town, unless such goose or gander be well-yoked with yoke 12 inches long, under penalty of impounding such goose or gander ; and goose or gander taken damage fesant shall pay five cents poundage fee." In 1798, with the consent of the town, the Legislature extended the limits of the city toward the East and West Rocks. Already the care of the poor was the chief burden upon the town. The first annual balance-sheet was entered in the "Town Records" for December, 1799, and out of a total expense of £630 the town's poor cost £514. The item had doubled in ten years.

With the opening year of the nineteenth century, the City Clerk was first instructed to act as the Clerk of the Common

Council.[1] The state of the public finances was constantly growing worse. The City Court was supposed to derive support
from the fines imposed therein, but the penalties were not carefully collected. A partial remedy for the defect was found in
1803, when the Common Council was empowered to appoint a
City Attorney.[2] The supply of water furnished another
troublesome question. A proposition to build an aqueduct was
first debated in City-Meeting in 1804. Two years later, the
consent of the General Assembly was received, and a committee, headed by Noah Webster, was elected to manage the
construction of an aqueduct. But poverty prevented the
successful termination of this effort, and compelled the city to
tolerate the inefficient service of creeks and wells. Unavailing were all endeavors to improve the quantity and quality
of the water in the East Creek.

PUBLIC LETTERS TO THE PRESIDENTS AND OTHERS.

A most peculiar feature of New Haven Town-Meetings at
this period were the eloquently-worded manifestoes upon
public affairs. Events of unusual interest and importance
could hardly fail to evoke a sermon or an eulogy from New
Haven. In 1793, five long resolutions assured Washington
that his policy of neutrality " Merits our warmest approbation and support," and that " We will exert ourselves to
promote a conduct friendly and impartial towards the nations
of Europe," etc., etc. In 1796, New Haven told the National
House of Representatives its opinion of Jay's Treaty: " We
view with great anxiety the opposition now attempted against
the treaty. . . . We avoid declaring what our decision might
have been, had this treaty been submitted to our determination. For us it is sufficient that we discover in it no
principles subversive of our Constitution."

---

[1] July 7, 1800.

[2] In 1815, the appointment of a City Attorney was, by law of the State,
vested in the City Court, and it has so remained.

At the close of John Adams's term of office, New Haven welcomed the homeward-bound ex-President and reviewed his administration with eulogistic words. Federalism reigned supreme in New Haven. "We view with abhorrence all attempts made in our country to mislead public opinion, to inspire distrust, to awaken a spirit of needless discontent, and to deprive magistrates, who have long and faithfully served the public, of their most grateful reward, the esteem and approbation of their constituents." Naturally enough, the community was soon embroiled with Thomas Jefferson, and favored him with frequent communications. His appointment of an aged citizen to the Collectorship has become a part of national history, but the most fruitful cause of correspondence was the embargo, or, as it was occasionally called in this vicinity, the "dambargo."   .

This measure completely killed a commerce which had not entirely succumbed to the unfavorable conditions of the Revolution. In 1787, 7,250 tons of shipping were registered in the port, and the amount had increased in 1800 to 11,000 tons. In 1790, the trustees of the famous wharf thought themselves justified in setting up a three-thousand-dollar lottery for the extension of their property, and they instructed Mr. Lyman, the taverner, "To increase hereafter at their meetings the quantity of his sling and toddy."

About 1792, the New Haven Bank was incorporated with a capital of $80,000, and the Chamber of Commerce began to meet in "Ebenezer Parmalee's front room, on the first floor." There were three shipyards, and, in the South Sea fleet, about a score of ships, three of which registered over 300 tons. The most famous of these was the *Neptune*, which, in 1799, brought home from a voyage around the world a cargo of tea, silk, and china, upon which the net profits were $240,000, and the duties upon which amounted to $67,000, or $20,000 more than the entire civil-list tax of the State.

The " Orders in Council " began the work of destruction. The brig *Anne,* bound homeward from a Danish port, was boarded twice by the French cruisers and three times by the English.   Everything edible was removed, and the captain, remonstrating with` a French officer, was told to eat pine shavings, "good enough food for Yankees."[1] If New Haven ships did not bring home many victuals, they were not so scantily provided with beverages ; for, in a couple of years, there passed through the Custom House two million gallons of rum, gin, brandy, and wines altogether.   It seems strange that any of the ships should have been meddled with, since they were provided with a formidably polite document which was called a " Municipal Letter," and which invoked in their aid the influence of the Mayor of New Haven.[2]

The year 1807 was marked by two events of memorable import in New Haven's development.   The First Methodist Church and Society were enabled to buy a lot for building purposes, and the embargo was declared.   The former sig-

---

[1] New Haven Historical Society Papers, III. : Ancient Maritime Interests of New Haven, by Thos. R. Trowbridge, Jr.

[2] The following is a copy of a "Municipal Letter" :

" Most Serene, Most Puissant, High, Noble, Illustrious, Honorable, Venerable, Wise and Prudent Lords, Emperors, Kings, Republics, Princes, Dukes, Earls, Barons, Lords, Burgomasters, Schepens, Counselors, as also Judges, Officers, Justiciaries, and Regents of all the good Cities and places whether ecclesiastical or secular who shall see these patents or hear them read, We, Samuel Bishop, Mayor, make known that the Master of the Catherine of 84 tons burthen, which he at present navigates, is of the United States of America, and that no subject of the present belligerent powers has any part or portion therein directly or indirectly ; and as we wish to see the said Master prosper in his lawful Affairs, our prayer is to all of the before-named and to each of them separately where the said Master shall arrive with his vessel, they may be pleased to receive the said Master with goodness, and treat him in a kind, becoming manner, permitting him upon the usual tolls and expenses in passing and repassing to pass, navigate, and frequent the Ports, Places, and Territories to the end to transact his business where and in what manner he shall think proper.   In which We shall be willingly indebted.

(Signed)   "Samuel Bishop,
                                        Mayor."

nalizes a turning-point in the long and unequal struggle
between the Orthodox Puritan and his dissenting brethren,
the brunt of which, in New Haven, was so long borne by
Trinity Church and by the inconsiderable band of Sande-
manians.   The embargo (December 22) resulted finally in
the transformation of New Haven from a commercial to a
manufacturing town.   During the year 1808, seventy-eight
vessels were shut into New Haven harbor.   In August, Elias
Shipman, Noah Webster, David Daggett, Jonathan Ingersoll,
and Thos. Painter, Esqrs., by order of the Town-Meeting,
prepared and forwarded to Thomas Jefferson a "Memorial"
of about 4,500 words, "Respectfully representing" that the
embargo ought to be modified or suspended.   One may note
the orthodox economy of this paragraph : "We are disposed
to foster the growth of manufactures as rendering the people
independent of foreign nations for articles of consumption,
but, in a country containing immense tracts of uncultivated
land, we question the policy of forcing into existence manufactures less congenial to the habits of our people than
agricultural pursuits.   Manufactures that are adapted to our
society will best thrive with unrestricted commerce."   This
faithful re-echo of the new economic gospel of that day should
be read in connection with Jefferson's letter in the same year
to his staunch supporter, Abraham Bishop, Collector of the
Port of New Haven.   The President has heard that "Col.
Humphreys, in your neighborhood," makes the best fine cloth
in the United States ; and, inasmuch as he desires to wear
homespun at the "New Year's Day Exhibition," he requests
Collector Bishop to forward a suit, and says that he will
deposit the price of it "with any member of the Legislature
here."[1]

   Jefferson returned, in September, a characteristic answer to
the memorial, alleging that no one knew better than himself
the inconvenience caused by the embargo.   He referred the

---

[1] New Haven Historical Society Papers, I. 143.

petitioners to the "Legislature" as the only authority competent to prescribe the course to be pursued. New Haven had its share, in the following winter (1809), in persuading Congress to defeat the Administration upon the question of limiting the duration of the embargo. The Town-Meeting of January 28 adopted a long series of resolutions breathing out the spirit of the subsequent Hartford Convention.[1]

"We will submit to national laws, consistent with the principles of the federal compact, and not repugnant to the spirit of the Constitution and to the fundamental principles of a free government."

" When the rulers of a free people transgress the limits of their authority, it is the right and duty of citizens to manifest a sense of injury and to seek redress."

The town solemnly declared the embargo to be a violation of the Constitution, quoted the Declaration of Independence, used such ominous expressions as " The insidious stratagems of peace become more terrible than the sanguinary operations of war," and " We must oppose the torrent of oppression." Finally there came an appeal to the Governor and Legislature to meet and take measures for the protection of rights. Subsequently the device of non-importation was found to be the same demon under a new name, and the town frequently cried out against it. The last memorial (in 1814) represented New Haven as " Already reduced to poverty and wretchedness."[2]

---

[1] In the winter of 1814–15. It assembled on the 14th of December, 1814.

[2] New Haven's share in the war of 1812 was not entirely confined to memorials. Mr. Trowbridge has related a laughable account of one privateering venture. In 1812, the sloop *Actress*, 60 tons, Capt. Lumsden, was fitted out in New Haven harbor as a privateer. In the Gulf Stream a big English ship was sighted, which was pronounced a tea-ship, and a veritable prize. Much elated, the crew of the *Actress* cleared for action, and were already drinking Jamaica rum in honor of their anticipated fortune. Capt. Lumsden arrayed himself in a resplendent blue suit, with red facings, and a cocked hat, lent him by Jeduthan Bradley, a Foxon militia captain. Capt. Lumsden hailed, and was answered, " The *Spartan*,

DOWNFALL OF FEDERALISM.

It would not be reasonable to suppose that these rebellious declarations were supported by the unanimous sentiment of the town. The unwavering Federalism of the official utterances was anything but popular in the taverns around Long Wharf, where the toast to "Free Trade and Sailors' Rights" was greeted with the greatest enthusiasm. But the minority in the town comprised more stable elements than sailors and laborers. We have seen how the Tory Episcopalian freemen came forward to assist actively in the formation of the city government. The freemen of whom these men were representatives, the freemen who, for one reason or another, were dissatisfied or at variance with the most flourishing Church in the community, fell easily into opposition to the first National Administrations, with which the major part of Connecticut heartily sympathized. Those men, therefore, who at first fought Federalism because they wanted to see the Government fail, "Who," as President Stiles wrote, "despised the Congress-Government," and most of whom despised also the New England Puritan idea, formed, together with those who antagonized Federalism on account of State pride or excess of republican zeal, the nucleus of the Anti-Federalist party in New Haven and in the State. But Toryism soon died away, and ecclesiastical heat availed only to keep alive the seeds of future political dissension. In the middle of President Madison's first term, the Democratic-Republican minority in Connecticut began to assume a more aggressive form, and in New Haven the omens of a new political birth were soon perceived.

---

of London." The name was ominous, for it belonged to a powerful frigate known to be on our coast. But, reflecting that this was a tea-ship, Lumsden said, "Consider yourself a prize to the U. S. privateer *Actress*. Send your papers aboard." The Britisher humorously asked Lumsden if he "Really expected a great ship like this to strike colors to such a little fellow." Lumsden swore, and threatened to fire, whereupon the *Spartan* displayed its sixty guns, and a voice said, "Come to our gangway, and we'll hoist you in."

The insolence of England, the prolonged supremacy of one party in the State and of another in the nation, the rights and wrongs of the various sects, the lack of a written Constitution for the State[1]—all these causes helped to produce and animate a body which first found an abiding mouthpiece and oracle on the 1st of December, 1812. Upon that day Mr. Joseph Barber issued the initial number of the *Columbian Register.*

In the spring election of 1813, New Haven gave the Administration ticket 59, out of 225 votes. During the two following years there was no contest, but in 1815 the *Register* took the lead in appealing to denominational jealousies, and, from that time on, the fight waxed warm, and extended from New Haven throughout the State. The minority adopted the name "Toleration Party," and professed to maintain the broad principles of equalization of all creeds before the law, and of equal rights for all men. The Toleration journals were filled with letters addressed to " Congregational Hypocrites," to " Downtrodden Episcopalians and Methodists." It was asserted that only Congregationalists had been elected to office, that Yale College and other Congregational institutions had been aided by public money, and that Episcopal schools and charitable foundations had been slighted and ignored. One indignant churchman informed the town through the columns of the *Register* that his vote would not again be cast for Governor John Cotton Smith. The Governor had deliberately walked across the Green to his boarding-place, when he might have accompanied some of his associates to Trinity Church to hear the Bishop preach.

The Federalist papers at first affected to despise the agita-

---

[1] A convention of Jeffersonian leaders at New Haven, Aug. 29, 1804, ventured to make the first noteworthy assault upon the venerable charter of 1662. Of what stupid tyranny the ruling party was capable may be seen in the fact that every justice of the peace who attended that convention was impeached before the next General Assembly.

tion. The *Journal* said that the Federalist party was in
no new danger from Episcopalian votes, " Because two-thirds
of the 2,000 Episcopalian voters in the State are and always
have been Democrats." But the apathy of the *Journal* was
of short duration. In the election of 1816, the Toleration
ticket was partially successful throughout the State. Hartford and New Haven for the first time gave Democratic
majorities, and the latter town elected Wm. Bristol as its
first Democratic Representative to the Legislature. It was a
stunning blow to the New Haven gentry, and it evoked the
following lamentation—written, as the *Register* said, " By a
half-fledged scribbler in the prostituted columns of the
Journal"—" O Shame ! Triumph of Apostacy and Delusion ! In this Federalist Town of New Haven, where four-
fifths of the Freemen are friends of order and steady habits,
prejudice, apostacy, and fanaticism are triumphant. The
result of the election this day furnishes the fullest evidence
that moral depravity and personal debasement form no
barrier to political delusion and sectarian prejudice. Oh,
Shame ! Judgment hath fled to brutish beasts, and men
have lost their reason."[1]

In the following year, there was a slight reaction in the
town. The Federalist ticket received thirty majority, which
the *Register* attributed to illegal votes cast by students and
tutors from Yale College, and to " The unexpected exertions
of four Congregational clergymen who attended and *voted at
the polls throughout the day*." But, in general, the Toleration-
ists went on from victory unto victory. Having gained possession of the State, and of most of the local boards as well,
they declared in favor of a written Constitution to replace
the ancient charter of 1662. The Federalists were put
upon the defensive, and in a hopeless cause, for the tide of
republicanism had now acquired an irresistible force. In
New Haven they seem to have absented themselves from

---

[1] The vote in New Haven was : Dem., 288 ; Fed., 200.

the Town-Meeting of December 29, 1817, which voted almost unanimously that the town's representatives should urge the immediate formation of a written Constitution. The *Register* said proudly that about two hundred voters attended, " Mostly mechanics," and it pilloried unmercifully a young Federalist lawyer who had ventured to ask that assembly, " Where are our most respectable citizens? Why are they not here ?"

In the summer of 1818 (July 4th), the Federalists of New Haven made a last vigorous effort to elect their own men to the Convention which was about to frame the new Constitution. One of their nominees was the Hon. James Hillhouse, the beautifier of the Green and of the city. Alluding to Mr. Hillhouse's agency in the removal of the graves from the Common, the *Register* exclaimed: " He is the most desperate and ferocious prosecutor of desperate and ferocious deeds. God forbid that the destroyer of the sepulchers of our fathers should ever receive the suffrages of their sons." The Democratic candidates were successful by a poll of 300 to 250, and in the next autumn the town ratified the new Constitution by a vote of 430 against 218.[1] New Haven Federalism was ended. The following eight years were years of political chaos. The Democratic body alone was a well-drilled, compact body, obeying without hesitation the commands of its half-dozen leaders. Only upon the question of slavery could an opposing majority be mustered in the town. Not until 1826 was the Whig party, which followed the standard of Clay, able to win its first victory in New Haven.

SLAVERY AND ABOLITION.

In the year after the adoption of the State Constitution, the town delivered, for the first time since the Revolution, an official utterance upon the subject of slavery.[2] The trumpet

---

[1] Records, VI. 62. In October, 1818. The Convention met in Hartford in August, 1818.

[2] December 27, 1819. Records, VI. 71, *et seq.*

gave no uncertain tone. The slave-power was seeking to gain both Florida and Missouri for degradation, and New Haven recorded its verdict substantially thus : " The existence of Slavery in the United States is, in the opinion of this meeting, an evil of great magnitude. It is the high and solemn duty of the government of this free and enlightened nation to prevent by all constitutional means the extension of Slavery. It is therefore

" *Resolved*, That, in the opinion of this meeting, the Congress of the United States has the undoubted right to prohibit the admission of Slavery into any State or Territory hereafter to be formed and admitted into the Union ;

" *Resolved*, That, in the opinion of this meeting, the admission of Slavery into any such State or Territory would be opposed to the Genius and Spirit of our government, and injurious to the highest interests of the nation ;

" *Resolved*, That the Senators and Representatives from this State in Congress be respectfully and earnestly requested to use their most strenuous exertions to prevent the further extension of Slavery in the United States."

So said the town ! Meanwhile the City-Meeting said not a word about the Missouri question. It was fixing the weight of loaves of bread at " The New York Assize," and the prices of the same by statute at 6¼ and 12½ cents—legislation surprisingly similar to Eaton's Assize of Bread in 1655. However, the time came when the city did speak, and to a very different purport from that of the foregoing.

In 1831, a number of Abolitionists, some of them residents of New Haven, subscribed funds for the establishment in New Haven of a college for the education of negro youth, and the promulgation of anti-slavery sentiment. Forthwith, as when, in Ephesus of old, a reform was proposed, the city was in an uproar. Mayor Dennis Kimberley[1] called a City-Meeting on the 10th of September. It was a crowded gathering, and adopted a long list of fiery preambles and

---

[1] He was a Whig.

resolutions which declared that "The propagation of sentiments favorable to the immediate emancipation of slaves,
and, as auxiliary thereto, the contemporaneous founding of
colleges for educating colored people, is an unwarrantable and
dangerous interference with the internal concerns of other
States, and ought to be discouraged; also that Yale College,
schools for females, and other educational institutions already
existing in this city are important to the community, but the
establishment of a college in the same place to educate the
colored population is incompatible with the prosperity if not
the existence of the present institutions of learning, and will
be destructive of the best interests of the city." Wherefore
the Mayor, Aldermen, Common Council, and freemen of the
city of New Haven mutually pledged themselves to resist the
establishment of the proposed college by every lawful means.
The Bourbons prevailed, and the project was abandoned.
Not long afterward the chivalrous citizens of Canterbury,
Connecticut, declared war on Miss Prudence Crandall because she was willing to teach "Niggers." Wm. Lloyd
Garrison, referring to "The proscriptive spirit," wrote: "The
New Haven excitement has furnished a bad precedent; a
second must not be given, or I know not what we can do to
raise up the colored population in a manner which their
intellectual and moral necessities demand." Ten years later
(1841), the town of New Haven appropriated $150 for a
school for colored children, and, in 1842, there were two such
schools.[1]

MUNICIPAL GROWTH.—SECTS.—ADMINISTRATIVE CHANGES.

During the rapid upspringing of the Democratic party
(1810–17), and amid the birth-throes of the new Constitution, political excitement seems to have checked even the

---

[1] Records, VI. 197. The captives of the famous *Amistad* were brought
to New Haven in 1839.

normally slow development of New Haven's municipal government. But with the winter of 1818–19 the symptoms of growth appeared again. Pressure of business caused the differentiation of a Board of Relief from the office of the selectmen. An increasing desire for official regularity in the place of previous easy informality manifested itself in a by-law by virtue of which the Common Council for the first time elected a sexton, a leader of the hearse, bell-ringers, and other officers necessary to the service of burial.

The 6th of July, 1820, was a red-letter day in the calendar of the First Methodist Church and Society. Their ambition to place their church by the side of its Congregationalist neighbors and within the jealously-guarded limits of the Green was gratified. The City-Meeting placed the seal of its final approval upon an ordinance permitting the Methodists to build an edifice upon the northwest corner of the public square.

Throughout the year the city government was engaged in framing a rudimentary Police Department. Night-watches were established, consisting of three superintendents and a score of watchmen, although the enabling act of the Legislature allowed seven superintendents and fifty watchmen.[1]

---

[1] That the city could exist thirty-six years without a regular force of this sort would seem to argue either Arcadian simplicity or alarming insecurity. The actual condition of affairs was probably a mixture of both. President Dwight, writing in 1810, depicted New Haven as a model Happy Valley, where disturbances were unknown, where private contentions hardly existed, and where ungirt Peace ruled alone. But one burglary had been known in fifteen years. However, he adds, "This good order of the inhabitants is the more creditable to them, as the police of the Town is far from being either vigorous or exact." At the risk of involving the worthy President in contradictions, it is worth while to compare another of his paragraphs with the foregoing. After dilating upon the excellences of the various social elements in New Haven, he says "The one considerable exception is the class of labourers. By this term I intend those men who look to the earnings of to-day for the subsistence of to-morrow. In New England almost every man of this character is either shiftless, diseased, or vicious. The local and commercial circumstances of this Town have allured to it a large (proportional) number of these men ; few of whom are very industrious; fewer, economical ; and fewer still, virtuous." (Travels, I. 193–4, 196.)

The work of renovation was continued into the year 1821.
The Fire Department was remodeled. The Fire Wardens,
who had held the entire responsibility, were now empowered
to elect a Chief Engineer and five Assistant Engineers.
Hereafter the Chief Engineer could order the demolition of
buildings, in order to prevent the spread of fire, without wait-
ing, as formerly, for the consent of the Mayor and the
majority of the Aldermen. The charter and its numerous
amendments were consolidated, and the Legislature recast
the charters of all the cities in the State into one Act. In the
same year a Baptist society followed in the path which the
Methodists had hewed out with such difficulty, and effected
a territorial lodgment. In the annual Town-Election, tithingmen were chosen for the Baptist and Methodist, as well as
for the Congregational Churches. Not until 1833 were the
first tithingmen elected for the Episcopal Church,[1] and the
Universalist and Roman Catholic Churches received this
token of official recognition in 1836.[2] In 1849, the town met
for special ballot, because it had omitted the election of tithingmen for the Society of Mishkan Israel, or, as the Town
Records put it, of " Miskin Israel."[3] The rapid increase in
the number of congregations must have rendered the choice

---

[1] Trinity Church had not needed tithingmen, if its worshippers were
generally as choleric as the one mentioned in N. H. Hist. Soc. Papers,
II. 38. Spying a little boy who was inclined to conduct himself
frivolously during the service, the devout Churchman rushed up to the
offender with the words, " You damned little rascal, how dare you behave
so in a church ? You thought you was in a Presbyterian meeting-house,
didn't you, hey ? "

[2] In this year each political party was accusing the other of sharp
practice in choosing a large number of tithingmen, who were by that
means qualified to become voters, and hence, it is to be supposed, party
workers. The trick had been in vogue for five or six years. At first the
Democrats had employed it successfully, but latterly the Whigs had beaten
the former at their own game. It is satisfactory to see that, in 1836, each
side was ashamed of the usage.

[3] The Town-Meeting was by law obliged to elect at least two tithingmen
in each congregation.

of tithingmen not only troublesome, but farcical. At the Town-Meeting of November 8, 1865, one hundred and twenty-five tithingmen were elected for thirty-one churches. After that year the selection of tithingmen was relinquished to the separate churches. The North, or United Church, still elects yearly two tithingmen, and other churches may do the same.

The Farmington Canal was an Old Man of the Sea for New Haven. It cut deeper into the financial prosperity of the place than into its soil. The Town-Meeting, which enthusiastically approved of the project, was appropriately held on the first of April, 1822. A few years later the city sunk in the Canal one hundred thousand dollars of borrowed money. The principal result of the investment was the rise in the rate of taxation to seventy mills on the dollar.

Moreover, in connection with a system of extensive borrowing, this extraordinary rate continued year after year. It was the inflation-period alike of nation, State, and city. In 1840, the tax was eighty mills on the dollar, while in 1846–47 the high-water mark was attained of ten cents on the dollar for ordinary city expenses, and an extra rate of two, in the second year three, cents on the dollar to pay for the fence around the Green. The town-rate during the same period was usually from two to three cents. It should not be forgotten, however, that these excessive rates were levied under Connecticut tax-laws upon an extremely small valuation of both real and personal property. Had the assessed valuation been more nearly equal to the real one, the same sums of money might have been raised by a really moderate tax. There seems to have been some distress caused by taxation, but it probably resulted from unfavorable conditions of trade, banking, and the currency, rather than from heavy rates. There was some very peculiar and happily unique tax-legislation by the City-Meeting of 1824. In order to provide the means for preserving the city from fire, the assessors were ordered to levy taxes principally upon the property of those citizens who had the most to fear from fire.

The Democratic phalanx, which had taken possession of the town under the standard of "Toleration," had been arbitrarily managed; and, during the second quarter of the century, the Whigs were generally predominant[1] in town and city. The growth of manufactures, encouraged by the long European wars, made Clay's "American System" popular in the community. But the political conscience of either party was then in its feeblest state. That insurgent, obstinate Democracy which we may call Jacksonism, asserting, against itself, unquestioning fealty to the will of a leader, infected both parties. As a result, almost every vestige of eighteenth-century aristocracy was gradually effaced. In 1826, the rising tide of Jacksonian Democracy left its mark upon the New Haven city government. An important amendment to the charter was obtained from the Legislature. The Mayor's term of office was hereafter limited to one year, and he was to be elected, with all other officers of the city, by ballot. Thus the chief officer of the municipality first became directly responsible to his constituents, and the hand of legislative authority was further removed. Hitherto the city offices had been generally held until death or old age incapacitated the incumbent. Under the new *régime*, offices were political prizes, and rotation was the order of the day. The peaceful atmosphere, which had previously seemed to linger even in the pages of the records, disappeared.

Henceforth the progress of urban development is more confused, more rapid, more tentative. The coming of the steamboat (1815) and the opening of the Canal (1828–1835) promised to make New Haven a distributing centre, and the necessity of improved means of local transportation seemed imperative. The roads of the town and streets of the city were in a wretched condition. The office of City Street Com-

---

[1] Their sway was practically unbroken, after 1834, until the dissolution of the party during Pierce's administration.

missioner had been created in 1818, and the Council had
then ordered sidewalks on the principal streets, but the City-
Meeting, three days later, vetoed the ordinance.

Not until 1834 was there a Superintendent of Sidewalks,
with orders to see that the sidewalks were leveled and properly paved at the expense of the property-owners. There
was persistent opposition. Although private individuals
had used pavements since 1809, a number of citizens who
were satisfied with the " good old times " seemed resolved to
sustain Dr. Manasseh Cutler's observation, in 1787, that the
streets were not paved and probably never would be. After
some years the city overrode the most violent protesters.[1]
More sympathy will be felt with the opinion of the people,
in 1833, relative to an Act of the Legislature authorizing the
selectmen of the various towns to sell for purposes of dis-
section the corpses of friendless paupers. The town strongly
repudiated this Act, and instructed its selectmen to bury at
public expense all such paupers who might pay the debt of
nature in New Haven. In 1835, both town and city revised
and improved their by-laws. Most of the changes and
amendments related to contested or defective elections, or
prescribed more rigidly the order of proceedings at the
annual elections. For some years thereafter, the names of
all freemen of the city who voted at the annual meeting were
copied into the city records. The First Selectman was still
the most important officer in New Haven, if size of salary is
any criterion. He received five hundred dollars a year,
while the Mayor was content with two hundred dollars.

The arrangement of the City Court, which had existed
since 1784, began to create dissatisfaction. Mayors and
Aldermen were now selected for political considerations, and
it was probably seen that a good partisan might not be a

---

[1] It is related that Wm. Lyon, who lived between Orange and State
streets, on Chapel street, when the city finally paved in front of his
dwelling, took long steps across the pavement and walked in the street,
declaring that " God's soil " was good enough for him.

learned judge. Therefore, in 1842, another amendment to
the charter[1] divested the Mayor and the Aldermen-Judges of
all judicial power and bestowed the same upon a new officer,
called the City Recorder, who was to be annually chosen by
the Common Council, and who was to receive one hundred
dollars per annum. This curtailment of the Mayor's powers
was made good in another direction. By virtue of his office
he was placed at the head of the Police Department. The
Recorder's Court had the same jurisdiction as its predecessor.
But there were conflicting interpretations of the real meaning
of the Act creating the Recorder's Court, so that Aldermen-
Judges were still elected, and could sit as side-judges with
the Recorder. In 1857, this usage was approved by a vote
of 661 to 561.

It had been voted, in 1836, that the City Watch should
serve both day and night. Three years later the labors of
the watchmen were, perhaps, somewhat lessened by the
return of the Fair Haven territory to the jurisdiction of the
town government. In 1842–3, the watch was costing the
city about two thousand dollars a year, and, apparently for
no other reason than this, there were determined attempts to
abolish the department altogether. In June, 1842, such a
motion was defeated by only three votes in a poll of two
hundred and seventy-five. One year afterward the City-
Meeting (October 14, 1843) actually instructed the Common
Council to discontinue the watch, and from that time until
1848 the city remained practically unguarded. An inadequate night-watch was employed, and in January, 1845, on
account of depredations by students and others, the Mayor
and Aldermen were commissioned to increase, at their discretion, the number of night-watchmen. Finally a series of
incendiary fires frightened the people back to complete sanity.

---

[1] In 1841, a series of letters appeared in the *Palladium* clearly and
forcibly criticising the construction of the city government. The advice
of this writer was almost literally followed in the next year.

A WINDFALL FROM WASHINGTON.

The resources of the town received a very material accession in 1837, as a consequence of folly in high places. On the 17th of January, the town voted that it would accept its proportion of the United States surplus deposited with this State, in accordance with the conditions imposed by the Legislature, appropriating the interest of such moneys to educational purposes. New Haven's share was the respectable sum of $27,427.67. It was forthwith loaned upon New Haven real estate, and the "Town Deposit Fund" has figured in each annual budget since.[1] Although this windfall was blown into New Haven's lap by a Jacksonian Administration, the town does not seem to have cherished Democratic statesmen very warmly. John Tyler was a Democrat, if he was anything. A City-Meeting was convoked June 17, 1843, to provide for his reception in New Haven, and a proposition to set apart $500 for his entertainment met this response:

" *Whereas,* It is expected that the President of the United States will pass through this city on his way from Bunker Hill to the Capitol; therefore,

" *Resolved,* That we recommend to the citizens generally to manifest in such manner as shall best accord with their own sense of propriety their respect for the office; nevertheless, without considering the embarrassed condition of the Treasury, the occasion does not require any pecuniary appropriation, or any action of the city in its municipal capacity."[2]

This was very cold comfort, especially when compared with the enthusiasm manifested a few years later (in 1848) over the prospect of a possible call from Henry Clay. The Mayor, at the head of a deputation of eleven citizens, was appointed

---

[1] Records, VI. 162.

[2] Jackson himself, in 1833 (June 15), met with a very ceremonious welcome to New Haven, and the *Herald* put "Jack Downing's Letter" side by side with the account of the President's reception.

to "Respectfully urge the venerable and illustrious statesman to come from New York to New Haven as the guest of the city."

But this was lukewarm when placed by the side of the long and well-written resolutions adopted upon the death of John Quincy Adams.

THE LIQUOR TRAFFIC.

With the beginning of the year 1840 the wires were laid for a temperance agitation, and with reason. Previous to that time the town had maintained a special license system.

January 10, 1840, free rum was introduced in the following by-law : "Voted, that all persons be allowed to sell Wines and Spirituous Liquors in the town of New Haven during the current year." This law was re-enacted from year to year. The results were naturally seen in the receipts of the courts and in the town balances. At the close of the fiscal year of 1839 there had been a balance in the treasury of $3,000 ; the grand jurors' fees for prosecutions amounted to $27 ; and the town tax-rate was at two cents. In 1843, the balance in the treasury was $301 ; the jurors' fees were nearly $1,000 ; and the town tax-rate had risen to three cents.

The state of affairs thus indicated could not fail to attract notice, and especially the attention of Mr. Charles B. Lines, a citizen of sleepless energy and abundant interest in public affairs. During 1843 and 1844 he conducted a brisk agitation in Town-Meetings for an abolition of the free-sale system. The question was transferred to legislative halls from 1845 to 1854, and finally a law was procured, essentially prohibitory in its intent, by virtue of which the towns might permit the sale of liquor through certain prescribed agencies, but only for sacramental, medical, or chemical purposes. Mr. Lines thereupon appeared in Town-Meeting, July 25, 1854, with a motion that all existing permissions for liquor-selling should be revoked, that the selectmen should hire some one agent to sell whatever liquor might be needed, and that they should be empowered to draw from the treasury for that purpose. Jonathan Stoddard, Esq., moved to table these resolutions, and his motion was carried by a vote of 803 to 671. The meeting then adopted a series of resolutions offered by Stoddard, to the effect that the selectmen might draw six and a quarter cents for the purpose mentioned, that the appropriation should take place in 1860, and that the money should be used in "The faithful execution of the law."

The first act had thus ended with the discomfiture of the temperance men; but Mr. Lines was not dismayed. Perhaps the fact that the town-tax had mounted to five and a quarter cents on the dollar aided him. On the 22d of August, 1854, he renewed his motion. Stoddard again opposed him and carried an adjournment for one year by a vote of 1,115 to 1,050. September 20, Mr. Lines repeated his motion, omitting the restriction of the selectmen to one agent. It was agreed that the town should take a day to ballot on the question. The 27th of September was fixed upon, and Mr. Lines was successful by 1,640 yeas against 1,407 nays. From that autumn until the spring of 1857, the report of the Town Liquor Agency was a feature of the annual Town-Meeting and of the annual Town-Budget. The books of the agent are preserved now in the Town Clerk's office, several neatly-kept volumes, in which the quarts or half-pints are entered opposite the purchaser's name, in the proper column of "Sacramental, Medical, or Chemical." It is perhaps needless to say that the "Medical" column is filled to overflowing. The Town Liquor Agency had another name in the mouths of the citizens, as appears by the action of the town on the 28th of November, 1856: "Voted, that Lucius Gilbert and Judson Canfield be a committee to investigate the affairs of the Town Agency, or Maine Law Grog-Shop, and report to the Selectmen." The Prohibitory System had been put on trial and had failed. The last sale of liquor in the "Maine Law Grog-Shop" is dated in February, 1857.

LIGHT IN THE STREETS.

Modern improvements were the order of the day in New Haven from 1840 to 1850. Steamboats had already come, and the Canal had impoverished the city. In 1848, the liberally-inclined citizens made up their minds to illuminate their ways with gas, and succeeded in forcing the city to do it by a vote of 182 to 80. The step was creditable to New Haven enterprise, for, at that time, Trenton, New Jersey, was the only other small city in the country which had put gas into its streets. The taxpayers who objected to the measure laid much stress upon the injury that the gas would work upon the trees, and in July, 1850, a committee was actually appointed to confer with the "President and Directors of the New Haven Gas Company with a view to ascertain what measures, if any, can be adopted to preserve the shade-trees of the city from the destructive action of the gas."

A HIGH SCHOOL.

During these years the schools of town and State were undergoing radical transformation, and were recovering from the low estate into which they had fallen in the earlier part of the century. The movement toward better things began in New Haven in 1844, when the First School District presented to the town resolutions advocating some provision for higher instruction and the formation of graded schools. The Town-Meeting consigned the subject to a committee, and the project ripened. In 1854 and 1855, graded schools were organized, and in the latter year the town elected its first Board of School Visitors. The re-organization of the New Haven School District under a Board of Education was completed in 1856.[1] Already official action by the School Society

---

[1] The towns were originally the educational units in Connecticut. But some of them were large, and contained outlying ecclesiastical parishes. In 1712, such parishes were allowed to direct their own schools. In 1717, they were authorized to lay taxes and choose school-officers. This was, practically, the formation of school-districts within the towns, although

in 1850 and 1852 had called into being the germ of a high
school, in connection with a grammar-school. The germ
became a developed organism in May, 1859, when the Hillhouse High School was established. In the same year the
familiar title, "Acting School Visitor" was dropped, and
"Superintendent of Schools" was substituted in its place,
but the duties of the office remained the same as before.
Since that time the increase of schools and of population has
promoted the gradual but steady enlargement of the Superintendent's responsibilities. The new school-system was
destined to struggle long for emphatic popular approval.
After seven years an unmistakable verdict was given. In
the spring of 1866, the Board of Education voted to recommend the discontinuance of the high school. In June, after
a thorough discussion, New Haven, as a School District,
decided to maintain the school by 1,170 votes against 449.

THE ERA OF RAILWAYS.

In our day of material forces widely subjugated to man's
use, there has been no industrial revolution more momentous

---

the selectmen were still the supervisors of all the schools. Moreover,
many of these parishes became towns, and, in general, the school-district
seemed to owe its genesis to the Church Society rather than to the town.
By the school-law of 1766 further subdivision of the towns into school-
districts was encouraged. The substitution of district for town-authority
was completed in 1798, and henceforth the town as an educational unit
was entirely superseded by the School Society. Supervision was transferred from the selectmen to specially-appointed officers, and the free high
schools, which had been by law maintained in New Haven and in the other
county towns, were no longer required.

The first backward step up this long-descending track was taken in
1838, by the creation of a supreme authority over the educational system
of the State. With some fluctuations of fortune, the centralizing influences have increased in strength from that day to this. A statute of 1866
allowed any town to abolish its districts and to revert to the original plan
of managing the schools as town-institutions. (See "Revised Statutes
of Connecticut"; and "Public Schools in Connecticut," by Henry E.
Sawyer, A. M., published in *Education* for Sept.–Oct., 1883.)

than the one wrought by the introduction of railways. Not
every town discovered the evils as well as the advantages of
railway-influence so quickly as New Haven did. The first
cars that ran in the city were on the Hartford Road in the
spring of 1839. In 1848, both the Canal Railway, as far as
Plainville, and the New York and New Haven Railway
were opened to the public, the former in January, the latter
in December. It was expected that the Canal Road would
be speedily completed to Springfield, Mass., and citizens of
New Haven who were inclined to be Micawberish expected
something to turn up that would be very big indeed. Over
the bed of the ill-starred Canal wealth would at last begin
to roll into New Haven. But the New Haven and Hartford
R. R. Co. had no mind to allow a parallel line, and it fought
its rival over every inch of ground, and with every weapon
that the arsenals of the law could furnish. The Hartford
Road made common cause with the owner of a bit of farm-
land which was included in the Canal Road's "lay-out" at
Simsbury. This man could "Neither be bought nor scared"
out of his comparatively valueless possession, which was
generally known as "The Peddler's Lot." The final result
was that the Canal Road never reached Springfield, and was
almost fatally crippled at the start. Indignation at New
Haven was at white heat, and, as usual at such times, Mr.
Charles B. Lines came to the front in the City-Meeting,
December 22, 1849, with nine long and fiery resolutions.
The flame of anti-monopolistic feeling in these resolutions
burns brightly enough to shed no little light in our own day.
" . . . . A railroad monopoly would be more odious than
the steamboat monopoly from which some of our citizens have
suffered so much. Therefore,

"*Resolved*, That the recent attempt by the New Haven
and Hartford Company to stop this important public work
at the very moment of its completion, after nearly a million and
a half of dollars had been expended upon it, and when only
one hundred rods remained to be finished, not less than the

stealthy manner in which the attempt was made, is an act of cunning and high-handed oppression, of doubtful legality, unworthy of honorable men, disgraceful to a corporation, and from the effects of which we appeal to the Legislature for relief."

Mr. Lines, always running a-tilt against the champions of evil, turned from rumselling and corporate selfishness to break a lance, or, more literally, to shoot bullets against the slave-power in Kansas. Times had changed since the day when a City-Meeting resolved to prevent the foundation of an "Abolitionist" college in New Haven. Meetings were held in the North Church to raise money and buy rifles for free-soil emigrants[1] to Kansas, and Mr. Lines became one of the leaders of a New Haven company which settled the county and town of Waubonsie.[2]

THE NEEDS OF THE POOR.

The day had now come when the moral sense of the community was shocked by the housing of criminals, paupers,

---

[1] Rev. Henry Ward Beecher gave them a parting address in the North Church, March 22, 1856.

[2] The community, therefore, was inevitably sundered to the very bottom by the Kansas quarrel. On the one hand, subscriptions were openly solicited for the purchase of "Kansas rifles," and on the other the *Register* spoke of 30,000 Connecticut Democrats ready to take up arms, if need be, to maintain the rights of the South. In the Presidential election of 1856, the town polled a large vote, out of which Fremont secured a small majority. In the following year, the Republican leaders imitated the ancient custom of the town, and opened an epistolary fire directly upon President Buchanan. A large assembly of citizens, in Brewster's Hall (July, 1857), addressed to the Chief Executive a memorial embodying their views of his duty to Kansas. Buchanan replied to them under date of August 15, 1857, and the memorialists rejoined September 22. The rejoinder was signed by many well-known men, among others by Rev. Drs. Nath'l W. Taylor and Leonard Bacon, Pres. Woolsey, Gov. Dutton, Mayor Skinner, Gen. Wm. H. Russell, Charles Ives, Eli Blake, James F. Babcock, and the Sillimans. The whole correspondence exhibited the points of the controversy in clear and vigorous rhetoric, attracted wide attention, and contributed largely to the formation of public opinion.

and lunatics under one roof.   The Rev. S. W. S. Dutton forcibly impressed upon the Town-Meeting of November 20, 1849, the disgrace of such an usage.   A committee, consisting of Messrs. Dutton, Wm. H. Ellis, Oliver Smith, Chas. B. Lines, and Prof. Benj. Silliman, was appointed to "Devise provision for the insane, disabled, and dependent poor, whom our laws consign to the Workhouse."   Mr. Lines moved that the selectmen should be instructed to "Remove immediately to the Insane Retreat at Hartford the insane persons now confined in the Almshouse."   The motion was approved, and the removals were made forthwith.   One year later (November 26, 1850), the committee reported that the old house had no conveniences nor sanitary advantages, and that the refractory could be confined only in small dungeons underneath the chapel.   The committee recommended the erection of a new Almshouse for the exclusive use of the "Virtuous Poor," and the town accepted their counsel.   It was the moral and material renovation of this period, rather than any sectarian feeling, which led the city to give to the Methodists, in 1848, five thousand dollars on condition that they would move their church-edifice away from the Green. The newly-developed solicitude for the city's beauty was curiously exemplified in the following ordinance: "Resolved, that that part of the Green now occupied by the Methodist Episcopal Society shall not be occupied by the students of any institution, or by any other individuals as a play-ground for playing ball or any other game of amusement."

THE CITY-MEETING.—CHARTER OF 1857.

The services which the water in the Canal had occasionally rendered in extinguishing fires probably emphasized the idea, in 1850, of a contract with the New Haven Water Company for a sufficient supply of water at all times for such purposes. This led to negotiations in 1852 for the purchase of the water-works by the city.   A vote in 1852 to buy the water-works was immediately succeeded by a counter-agitation, which was successful in the next year. The water-supply was abandoned to the care of the private projectors, but the subject was not laid away to rest before 1856, and ended in successful lawsuits against the city. The City-Meetings held to decide the matter were tumultuous, and were open to suspicions of chicanery. The tellers were unable to count the votes, and the Mayor was unable to preserve order.

Such disorders turned the public attention toward additional reforms in the government. In 1853, the city was divided into four wards, and the ward organization was still further perfected in 1857, when the four wards were replaced by six. But the centre of discussion was the cumbrous institution of the City-Meeting. It was plain that the size of the city rendered government by such a democratic assembly difficult, if not impracticable. Yet so great was the distrust of the few by the many, that the City-Meeting in 1849 forbade the appropriation by the Common Council of more than one hundred dollars without the approval of a City-Meeting called for that purpose.

There was good sense enough in the city to repeal the law shortly afterward, but it was a sign of rapid progress that, in the spring of 1854, the following motion prevailed in City-Meeting: " Resolved, that the Mayor, Aldermen, and Common Council be requested to digest a constitution or plan of government for the city of New Haven to be submitted to the citizens, by which all the powers now vested in the municipal corporation, styled ' The Mayor, Aldermen, Common Council, and Freemen,' shall be vested in a representative body, or bodies, to be chosen by electors residing in the city of New Haven; and that the same be prepared and submitted in season to be passed upon in City-Meeting, and, if approved, to be carried to the Legislature for its sanction."

The motion was the germ of a new charter which received legislative sanction in 1857. The Mayor and Common

Council were no longer fettered, as they had been, by the City-Meeting,[1] and the duties of the Council were materially increased. Among the various propositions for reform, the plan of abolishing the two-headed system of Town and City-Government did not escape consideration. Both town and city, the former leading the way, appointed committees in 1852 to confer together upon the feasibility of uniting the two jurisdictions under one administration. The only result of the conference was, perhaps, the discontinuance of the separate Town-Meeting for the election of town-officers. This alteration was adopted November 12, 1855. Henceforth town-officers were elected by districts, at voting-places designated by the selectmen. The practical effect was to make town and city voting-places the same so far as the city extended.

TOWN-OFFICERS.

The Town-Agent, measured by his present duties and powers, is a modern growth upon the ancient trunk of town-government. But though the special importance of the office is of recent date, its beginnings can be traced far back in the town's history. The general power to sue for the town was bestowed upon the townsmen in December, 1700. Even before that time the oversight of the poor had been enrolled among their responsibilities. Throughout the eighteenth century the townsmen, as a body, performed such offices, or delegated the labor to some of their own number. In the first years of the nineteenth century, the town at its annual meeting usually divided the Town-Agency between two of the selectmen, and, for the first time, bestowed upon each the title "Town-Agent." For example, in 1800 the First Selectman, Jeremiah Atwater, was appointed an agent to sue

---

[1] The provisions were: "Within 60 days from the passage of a bye-law the Mayor *may* call, and, upon written request of 7 Common Councilmen and of 20 other freemen, he *shall* call a City-Meeting to approve or reject said bye-law." But from this date the City-Meeting slumbered.

and to be sued for the town, while Thomas Punderson, the Second Selectman, was chosen the Town-Agent to take care of the poor. The usage varied; sometimes the First Selectman was not a Town-Agent, and sometimes the Board of Selectmen, as a body, was Town-Agent. Subsequently the Board of Selectmen appointed as Town-Agent one of their own number, usually the one who was also named First Selectman.

Political complications caused each party to adopt, in 1878, the custom of designating upon the town-ticket the candidate for Town-Agent, thus ensuring a direct election by the people. This is a device intended to render the office more popular in its character, and also more secure to the party in power. The law of the State seems to give the Board of Selectmen a choice in the matter; but the present incumbent of the office and his party-friends have refused to permit the board to vote, alleging that the popular election is sufficient. Since 1848 the Town-Agent has received a larger compensation than any other town-officer. Since that time, also, the great increase in the foreign-born population has added largely to his responsibilities. The annual distribution of considerable sums for what is called " Outdoor Relief" is virtually under his control. These facts have given the Town-Agent a certain hold upon a large body of voters, and have made him an influential factor in town-politics.

The Town-Clerk, after 1847, earned two hundred dollars per annum, an increase of one hundred per cent. upon his previous compensation. The salary of the First Selectman was raised in 1848 to eight hundred dollars,[1] while the Mayor

---

[1] In December, 1812, the selectmen were first authorized to draw pay for the time devoted to the public service. Down to the time of the Civil War, the selectmen cared for all the highways throughout the town, yet Captain Beecher, through the greater part of his sixteen years of service, received but five hundred dollars a year, and furnished his own horse and wagon. His predecessor, Squire Mix, furnished the same, and obtained only a dollar a day.

and City Clerk, six years later, were drawing but five hundred dollars each. With the approach of war-times, salaries rapidly rose, until they attained more nearly to the modern standard. In 1860, the Mayor and City Clerk respectively obtained one thousand, and eight hundred dollars.

CITY-IMPROVEMENT.—POLICE AND FIRE DEPARTMENTS.

In this year the first steps were taken toward a city-sewerage system. The attention of the authorities was forcibly arrested by a suit which Samuel Peck brought against the city for damages on account of municipal neglect to provide sewers. The city could previously boast of a few small sewers, but there was no adequate provision for drainage; and not until ten years after this, during Mayor Lewis's first administration, was the sewerage system made thorough and complete. The spirit displayed in the Common Council in 1861, over the construction of the George-street sewer, may explain some of the hindrances to prompt and effective action.

It was ordered that, in accepting bids for building the sewer, " No contract should be made with any person not a citizen of New Haven, and that the whole work, so far as practicable, should be in the hands of New Haven citizens." Councilman Healey tried to add a provision that each laborer employed should be paid at least one dollar a day.

From the time of the introduction of railway traffic and competition (in 1848) until the breaking out of the war was a period of active expansion. Increasing business demanded a more practical administration of public affairs. Hence came those attempts which have been recounted to divide, define, and restrict official functions, to simplify and improve antiquated methods. Yet progress was, after all, exceedingly slow. The forward step was taken painfully and, as in the case of the city-sewerage, with tedious delay. No straw shows more plainly the adverse direction of the prevalent

wind than the fact that, until 1861, horses and cows were
pastured in the streets within the city-limits without much
efficient hindrance from the authorities. But in that year
the energy of one man, James F. Babcock, caused the adoption of a stringent by-law, which was finally successful in
abating the nuisance. Three or four years earlier it had been
a recognized custom to entrust scavenger-duty in the gutters
to swine, and the constables who served orders for the demolition of pig-pens within the city-limits are said to have
seriously endangered their chances for re-election thereby.
Mr. Babcock might not have been so successful in his crusade
against vagrant cattle, had not the same year of 1861 wit-
nessed the replacement of the old Department of the Watch
by a more modern Police Department. This reform, and
the transformation of the Fire Department, were the two
most important municipal changes that immediately pre-
ceded the war. The City Government and the Legislature
concurred in 1861 concerning the organization of a new
police force, under a board of six Police Commissioners, with
terms of three years each. In June, 1862, Chief-of-Police
Pond made his first annual report. The police cost the city
that year ten thousand dollars. Chief Pond objected to the
Legislature's restriction of the number of policemen to
twenty, and it seems that the obstacle was soon removed.

The Fire Department was remodeled at the same time and
upon the same plan. A board of six Fire Commissioners
was created, and the Chief Engineer and his subordinates
placed under its control. The new companies were, of course,
paid for their services. The former volunteer companies had
become centres of political influence, not always of the better
sort, and in some cases they even wielded a degree of social
power. They were disbanded in the summer of 1861, and in
June, 1862, the commissioners entered upon their duties.

In connection with the development of the Fire Department, mention may be made of a remarkable petition which
was presented to the Common Council in 1865 by Henry

Peck, Theodore D. Woolsey, *et al.*[1]   The petitioners besought that a mutual city-insurance system might be adopted whereby every building within the city-limits should be insured by the city.   The property-owners were to be "Taxed at an amount not to exceed in any instance what was paid to the insurance companies."   The request was supported by elaborate calculations of the profits of insurance companies which might thus be saved to the citizens.

The petition was referred to the Fire Department Committee of the Common Council, who reported favorably upon it, alleging that 12½ per cent. upon a total valuation would cover all losses and leave a profit to the insurers.   The danger of a great fire in the city was not regarded as imminent enough to render the scheme impracticable.   The Common Council, after delay, instructed the committee to apply to the Legislature for an act authorizing the city to become its own insurer, but stipulated that no such act should take effect until it had been ratified by a City-Meeting. Nothing more is heard of the proposal.   This was the most noteworthy spurt of socialism in the whole course of New Haven's municipal career.   Nothing could be more directly opposed to the general tenor of the political philosophy of the community.

IN THE CIVIL WAR.

When the war-cloud of 1861 began to hide from view all matters of municipal and local interest, New Haven, as in 1776 and 1812, contained a strong conservative party opposed to bold measures and desiring pacific discussion.   A petition from New Haven was forwarded to Congress, in 1860, asking for peace-legislation, in order to satisfy the border slave-States.   When the echoes of the guns fired upon Fort Sumter reached New Haven, the *Register* said, "Henceforth these States pass into two Republics instead of one."

---

[1] The late Hon. William W. Boardman is said to have been chiefly responsible for the project.

After Bull Run there was much ill-suppressed feeling upon both sides in the city, and some of the more outspoken friends of the South were kept under surveillance. On the other hand, there was prompt support of Lincoln's administration by the more loyal portion of the population. Volunteers speedily offered themselves, and meetings of the citizens chose committees to procure supplies and forward the work of enlistment.[1] Persons securing recruits were paid by the citizens' committee three dollars for each recruit. The city appropriated money for bounties, and for the support of families of volunteers.

In the spring of 1861, a Home Guard was formed with about four hundred members, some of whom afterward saw service at the front. In 1862, the call for 300,000 volunteers aroused earnest effort in New Haven. A bounty of one hundred and seventy-five dollars was óffered. The first Town-Meeting to take official cognizance of the necessities of enlistment was held on the 5th of August, 1862. Resolutions offered by the "National Committee" were adopted, beginning "Whereas, the President of the United States has called for 300,000 volunteers to aid in putting down a causeless war," and enabling the treasurer to borrow $75,000 for the payment of bounties. The issue of town-bonds to the value of $180,000 was also authorized. But the enlistments were not numerous enough, and, in State and nation, men began to speak of a "Draft." New Haven's quota was 662. Up to September 1 there had been 319 enlistments. Resolutions offered in the September Town-Meeting to facilitate the coming draft were opposed by Mr. James Gallagher, and were rejected.

Partisan feeling became so violent that it was deemed best to send a committee from New Haven to Washington to

---

[1] See Crofut & Morris's Military and Civil History of Connecticut during the War of 1861–65. The first citizens' mass-meeting to consider the perilous state of the country was held in Brewster's Hall in 1861, on the historic date of the 19th of April.

request the arrest and confinement of all persons discouraging the enlistments. In the summer of 1863, the draft came, and, for a short period, New Haven was threatened with riot. The same party-violence that shed blood in the streets of New York during those dreadful July days appeared in New Haven also, but was overawed by the firmness of the authorities. On the 23d of July, the Town-Meeting passed by-laws to relieve the harsher features of the draft. The principal amelioration was in the vote that the town would hereafter purchase exemption for any conscript whose family necessities required his presence at home. In January, 1864, the selectmen were authorized to pay three hundred dollars to set free any citizen from enrollment. The town was generous with money during this year, and voted large sums for the purposes of the war.

No picture of official action can do justice to the share that New Haven as a whole took in these troublous times. The reactionary and even disloyal element left its impress necessarily upon the record of municipal effort, and yet New Haven was liberal with money and supplies, and the stream of contribution ceased only with the close of hostilities. To-day, the town counts high upon its roll of fame the honored names of such heroes as Theodore Winthrop and Alfred H. Terry.

Recent Charters.

The charter of 1869 marks a culminating point in New Haven's constitutional development. In size, spirit, and organization it began to be in reality a modern American city. Prior to that time it was a more or less thriving, overgrown village. Between 1850 and 1880 the city's population increased threefold, its grand list eightfold. With the formation of a paid fire department and of a police force worthy of the name in 1861–62, the municipality put forth signs of maturing strength, and commenced to reach upward and outward for a wider sweep.

Old forms of administration were outgrown and outworn, while experience gradually demonstrated the full range of municipal rights and duties. The charter of 1869, as usual, extended the sphere of the City Council's activities, but its most important provisions affected the judiciary.

The Recorder's Court was amended out of existence. In its place, and in place of the old-fashioned Justice's Court which had up to this time been the Police Court of the city, was substituted "The City Court of New Haven." Jurisdiction, therefore, was granted to it in both civil and criminal cases. The sole power of choosing the two judges of the new court was lodged in the General Assembly. As before, the City Attorney was to be the appointee of the court, but he no longer performed the duties of legal adviser to the city. That service was transferred to the corporation counsel, henceforth the best remunerated officer in the city government. The annual city-elections were hereafter to be held on the first Monday in October, and the municipal and calendar years were made coterminous. At the same time the city extended its boundaries by annexing the Fair Haven peninsula between Mill and Quinnipiac Rivers—an act which was consummated on the 5th of July, 1870. The town replaced its loss, eleven years later, by the annexation of territory to the eastward, whereby it gained completer control over the waters of its harbor.

The growth of the city necessitated a readjustment of the ward system. Ten wards were created in 1874, and the number was increased in 1877 to twelve. It was a slight counterbalance to these advances that, in 1873, New Haven unwillingly lost its honors as a capital, while Hartford regained the position that it had held in the 17th century.

The fifth and latest city-charter, that of 1881, has placed the city election upon the first Tuesday in December. The hope was that thus the quadrennial excitements of national party strife might be excluded from local elections. The charter of 1881 was intended also to improve the arrangement of the various departments, especially by ensuring equal representation of the two political parties upon the Boards of Commissioners. The previous influence of unscrupulous partisanship in departmental administration made the need of some remedial effort seem urgent.

CONSERVATIVE INFLUENCES IN THE COMMUNITY.

The gradual growth of municipal power has exhibited in succession many slowly-shifting phases. Though changes must be, yet, through them all, come glimpses of a typical, fundamental conservatism. For nearly a quarter of a millennium the town and region of New Haven have preserved a local character, a well-defined individuality, separate from those of other old colonial centres.

Its political affiliations have strengthened rather than diminished its exclusiveness. In 1639, it received at the hands of Davenport and Eaton the impression of an ultra political and religious conservatism, of ambitious commercial enterprise, and of zeal for education. Under the heat of adverse fortune the vision of commerce melted away, but the belief in the destiny of New Haven as a port for traffic, though intermittent, endured.

It seemed on the point of realization at the beginning of this century. That hope faded; yet the city has kept a stronger grip upon commercial life than many of its quondam rivals along the New England coast, and it occupies to-day a respectable rank among the national harbors.

Connecticut's laws, in 1664, could abolish the official but not the popular conservatism. Davenport's church was still "The famous Church of New Haven," the stronghold of purest orthodoxy, proud of its early distinction as one of the few New England churches framed on the apostolic model, with a complete presbytery within itself. The course of the Church, the real core of the town, is more significant of the local feeling in the ancient day than the quiet development of the secular government. It is not surprising, therefore, to find Davenport's church a stickler for pure Congregationalism long after the more radical brethren of Connecticut and Massachusetts had leaned more and more toward the Presbyterian or "Parish way." Hooker's church, at Hartford, was thus split in 1669.

The New Haven Church was once again on the conservative, orthodox side during the quarrelsome days of the Saybrook Platform (1708), and although the New Haven pastor, Pierpont, was a master-builder of that platform, his church sent no delegates to the synod and held aloof from its conclusions.

In the great awakening of 1741, the shibboleths had changed, and the Saybrook Platform now meant Orthodoxy, while the "New Lights" were Calvinist and Radical Reformers. The New Haven Church, in 1742, therefore, ranged itself for the first time under the Saybrook banner. The progressive minority rejected this action as "Contrary to the known fundamental principle and practise of said church time out of mind, which has always denied any juridical or decisive authority under Christ, vested in any particular persons or class, over any particular Congregational Church."[1]

So the first division in the religious community was proclaimed in the name, not of new truth, but of conservative traditions. The tendency of New Haven's ecclesiastical thought and custom has steadily retained its primitive character. It has been slow-moving, soon solidified, tenacious of past modes and traditions, backward in admitting change or in recognizing new movements. Society in general, both lay and clerical, has moved along slowly and ponderously in the rear rank, gaining perhaps in wide outlook and the judicious adaptation of means to ends, but possibly losing also in early fortune and in enthusiasm.

Some light has now been cast upon the causes which have

---

[1] Trumbull, II. 842.

made Yale College so conservative; yet it should not be forgotten that the institution has also reacted upon its environment as a promoter of permanence. It is not necessary to dwell upon the events of 1744, when the college made war upon Locke's essay upon " Toleration " and expelled two students for attending a Separatist meeting in a private house. The events were the fruits of a bitter and extraordinary controversy. But Yale has brought to New Haven a scholastic atmosphere unfavorable to a normal political and social development, and a population which has cared everything for the administration of the college, little or nothing for that in the City Hall. All these peculiar influences were particularly potent while the town was small, and they have increased with the city, though not proportionally.

Until a recent day, the best interests of the city have suffered because so many of its most intelligent residents were men who looked upon the affairs of the community as foreign to their world; who may have been profoundly interested in Roman politics of the time of Cæsar, or even in national politics of their own day, but who overlooked the civic structure which immediately contained and concerned them. There are numbers of people who have made New Haven their home in order to facilitate the education of their children, or in order to enjoy for themselves the privileges and sentiments of a university neighborhood. Such motives do not frequently underlie an active participation in the duties of good, energetic citizenship. Still it must not be forgotten that this relation of a life of " slippered ease " to the duties of a citizen involves but one aspect of the town's common life. Where New Haven, as a university town, has lost in one direction, it has gained a thousandfold in many others. In its political development, the Town-State is only one among many; through its identification with Yale the community has exerted an educational influence unique and far-reaching.

In the political world, also, New Haven's long unbroken,

slowly-changing party majorities have illustrated her claim to a large share in the inherited title of Connecticut, "The Land of Steady Habits." In 1800, as in 1770, it was the cities and trading centres of the State that held back the more radical country-districts. New Haven, like the major part of New England, passed unmoved through the national awakening of the West and South in 1808–16. The final overthrow of Federalism was achieved by confounding it with Congregationalism and attacking it—first, as a denomination, secondly, as a political party. The town remained, indeed, for twenty years under Whig domination. The old conservatism had been mostly broken down, the new conservatism had not yet arrived; but the anti-slavery sentiment, which had been so pronounced in the era of the Revolution, was counteracted by the multiplication of commercial relations, and found a feebler and feebler utterance after the narcotic compromises had weakened the moral strength of the whole country. With the beginning of railway connections, in 1848, came the crowds of Irish and other foreign laborers, and the political balance slowly, steadily indicated the growing preponderance of the untrained voters.

The rivalry between New Haven and Hartford means much more than commercial competition between two urban populations. It is the contention of regions rather than of cities. It is traceable through the whole history of the State back to the charter-quarrel of 1662–64, when one colony was pitted against the other. Waymarks of the struggle that ensued for supremacy within the colony are recognized in the accession of New Haven to the honors of a capital town in 1701, and in the acrimonious disputes over the final settlement of Yale at New Haven in 1717;[1] afterward, common knowledge recalls the unceasing competition between the cities, terminating, perhaps, in the "Single-Capital" contest of 1873. That dependence of the former New Haven Colony

---

[1] The two cities were also among the active competitors, in 1822, for the possession of the future Trinity College.

upon New York, which geographical location necessitated, was further encouraged by these successive animosities. If a line be drawn diagonally across the State from the north-west corner to the mouth of the Connecticut River, the towns and cities to the west of that line are found to rest upon New York as an economic and social basis, just as those upon the east side derive their inspiration from Boston. Of the former of these tracts New Haven is the capital; of the latter, Hart-ford. This division of influences should be borne in mind when we read that, in the Revolution, New Haven and Fairfield Counties contained many Tories, while the eastern part of the State was almost unanimously patriotic; that a Windham County mob forced the New Haven stamp-dis-tributor to resign in 1765; and that, one hundred years later, it was, as usual, the Hartford end of the State, the eastern counties, which held the State firmly for Nation with a big " N," and neutralized by steady and large majorities the conservative, oligarchical, pseudo-democratic tendencies of Southwestern Connecticut.

VOTERS OF NEW HAVEN CITY

Elect
- By Wards .. The Court of Common Council ..
- At Large { Mayor. Treasurer. City Clerk. Auditor. Sheriff.

36 Councilmen elect { 2 Commissioners of Finance. 1 Clerk. 1 Page.

24 Aldermen elect... { 4 Commissioners of Finance. 6 " Public Works. 6 " Police. 6 " Fire Department. 1 Page.

COURT OF COMMON COUNCIL conjointly

Elects
- Corporation Counsel.
- Asst. City Clerk.
- 144 Jurors of the City Court.
- 3 Members each for Boards of Compensation.
- Any Number of Special Constables.
- Needed Number of Weighers, Measurers, Surveyors, and Inspectors.
- One or more Inspectors of Gas Meters.
- " " " Water "
- Sealer of Weights and Measures.
- 3 Supervisors of Steam Boilers.
- Janitors. Bath-house Keepers.

COMMISSIONERS OF PUBLIC WORKS elect
Supts. of Streets, Sewers, and Public Parks, City Engineer, and all Employees on Roads, Bridges, Sewers, and Parks.

COMMISSIONERS OF POLICE elect
Chief of Police—appoints Supervisor of Vehicles. All Members of Police Department.

COMMISSIONERS OF THE FIRE DEPARTMENT elect
Chief Engineer and Assistants. Fire Marshal " Supt. of Fire Alarm Telegraph, and all Officers and Men of the Department.

THE MAYOR

Names
- And Court of C. C. confirms { The Coroner. 3 Commissioners Municipal Bond Sinking Fund. 3 " Sewerage " " 3 Commissioners of Public Buildings.
- And Aldermen confirm .... { 2 " East Rock Park. 6 Members of Board of Public Health.

Nominates—to the Aldermen their Standing Committees on { Buildings. Licenses. Numbering Streets. —chooses Clerk and Inspector.

The Mayor and the President of the Board of Councilmen nominate to the Court of Common Council, its

Joint Nominating Committee, which nominates the Joint Standing Committees on ....
Annual Reports. Appropriations. Auditing. Bath Houses. Building Lines. Claims. Commercial and Manufacturing Interests. Fire Department. Nominations. Ordinances. Printing. Railroads and Bridges. Retrenchment, Reform, and Abuses. Sewers. Squares. Streets. Water.

Board of Public Health—elects Health Officer and Assistants.
Supervisors of Steam Boilers—elect Inspector.
Sealer of Weights and Measures may name, and Court of Common Council—appoint Assistant Sealers.
Harbor Commissioners—elect Inspector and Clerk.
Various Boards, in general, elect their own Clerks.
Citizen-Donors of East Rock Park elect, and the Mayor confirms—3 Park Commissioners.

THE LEGISLATURE
Elects { 6 Harbor Commissioners. Clerk of City Court. The Judge of the City Court—appoints { Asst. Clerk of City Court. Asst. " " " City Attorney.

City Attorney appoints, and the Judge confirms—Asst. City Attorney.

VOTERS OF NEW HAVEN TOWN, including City,

Elect, at large........
- 7 Selectmen.
- 1 Town Agent.
- Town Clerk.
- Tax Collector.
- Treasurer.
- Registrar of Vital Statistics.
- 2 Town Auditors.
- 2 Registrars of Voters.
- 3 Sealers of Weights and Measures.
- 5 Assessors.
- 5 Members of Board of Relief.
- 5 Managers of Town Deposit Fund.
- 5 Pound-keepers.
- 5 Haywards.
- 6 Grand Jurors.
- 7 Constables.
- 7 Surveyors of Highways.
- 7 Fence-viewers.
- 7 Gaugers and Inspectors.
- 9 Packers.
- 9 Weighers.
- 56 Justices of the Peace.

Voters of New Haven School District elect—9 Members of Board of Education.

Board of Education makes all School appointments.

Selectmen choose—Clerk.

Heads of Departments choose—Clerks and Assistants.

Two Years' Term for
- Mayor.
- City Clerk.
- Auditor.
- Sheriff.
- Aldermen.
- 4 Commissioners of Finance.
- Corporation Counsel.
- Sealer of Weights and Measures.
- Officers of the City Court.

Three Years' Term for
- Coroner.
- Commissioners of Public Health.
- "   "   " Works.
- "   " Police.
- "   " Fire Department.
- Board of Education.
- Supervisors of Steam Boilers.
- Harbor Commissioners.

By City Charter, the Town Tax Collector's Department has common jurisdiction over Town and City. The same person is, customarily, Town and City Treasurer.

The Mayor is President of the Boards of Aldermen and Finance, and ex-officio Chairman of the Commissions of Public Health, Works, Police, Fire Department, and of the Park Commission.

Removal of Commissioners is possible only by a two-thirds vote of the Aldermen, except that the Mayor may remove for cause any Park Commissioner chosen by the citizen donors.

The City's supply of gas and water is controlled by private companies. New Haven has, by vote, refused to deprive the Water Company of its monopoly.

II.

THE PRESENT MUNICIPAL ADMINISTRATION.

"'To the end it may be a government of lawes, and not of men."
—Massachusetts "Body of Liberties," 1641.

The spirit of moderation which has generally been dominant in New Haven has ensured to the municipality a
constitutional development that is, at least, continuous.
There has been no succession of brand-new city charters of
diverse patterns, such as have been bestowed upon New
York.

On the contrary, the first charter has afforded a kernel to
all the others, and reform has been sought by amendment
rather than by substitution. Efforts to condense and simplify
have stopped short of the limits that might have been attained.
The praiseworthy tendency to hold firmly to the past lends a
line along which future development, if healthy, must take
place. Every analysis of existing forms should give due
weight to this municipal growth by cell-formation.

The School District.

Besides the town fabric, New Haven Township contains
school-district, city, and borough organizations.[1] As a
school district, the greater part of the town[2] is under the
control of nine men who compose the Board of Education.

---

[1] The borough of Fair Haven East is a minor municipality whose operations are foreign to this inquiry. However. in order to complete the view
of the town's official structure, it may be said that the borough elects
annually, on the second Monday in May, six burgesses, three assessors, a
clerk, bailiff, treasurer, collector, and a warden.

[2] New Haven School District includes all the township excepting West-
ville, and a small district at South End.

Members of the board serve without salary for three years, and three are chosen yearly. They are elected neither upon city nor town tickets, but a special election-day is devoted to them. Their powers are large. The board appoints a Secretary, a Superintendent of Schools, and all the teachers and assistants in all the schools. The position of the Board of Education in the school district is similar to that which the Board of Selectmen holds in the town. It manages the district's affairs, and is amenable only to the voters of the district in school-meeting assembled. In this meeting, comprising usually but a handful of people, the amount of the annual taxation for school purposes is determined upon the basis of the estimates made by the board. In the tax bills the school tax is reckoned by itself, but its collection is entrusted, with the usual formalities, to the common financial officers. The Board of Education maintains committees upon finance, schools, and school buildings, and may be said to unite administrative with legislative functions. The majority of those who have directed New Haven's educational progress has wrought with singleness. of purpose for the good of the schools, and has extended over them the care that only ability, interest, and long experience could provide. Under their oversight the district has obtained remarkably efficient schools and good school buildings, without accumulating any considerable indebtedness. Although the danger that party-spirit would dictate the election of unworthy men to the board has been possible rather than probable, yet the exigencies of popular elections have occasionally supplied the board with factious and fractious members.

The Superintendent, who is the board's chief subordinate, finds his intimate relations with his superiors and with the schools sources of perplexity. If he establishes a cordial understanding between himself and the board, and exerts himself to improve the administration of the schools, the cry of "One-man-power" is raised. Promotions among the teachers are hampered by resort to political influence and by claims for locality-representation. The latter result of our practical politics has produced some absurd phenomena in New Haven. In the summer of 1885, the Superintendent and the majority of the board agreed to call a teacher from a neighboring city to preside over one of the New Haven grammar schools.

Politicians, small-minded men, and even reputable newspapers, raised a windy protest against " Inviting an outsider to come and live on New Haven taxpayers." This folly might be deemed exceptional, 'if it had not occurred in the same community that, twenty years ago, favored the employment of " New Haven laborers only " upon a sewer. Such disadvantages naturally attend a democratic supremacy, and must be endured. One improvement in the existing condition of affairs seems practicable, and that is the lengthening of terms of membership upon the Board of Education. There is no reason why men who are qualified to serve in this capacity should not be elected for six years instead of three.

Greater permanence in school government would be a positive advantage. Above all things, the Superintendent should feel assured of a steady supporting influence for as long a time as possible.[1] His tenure of office is determined by the board, and has of late been fixed at two years; but in 1886 the board saw fit to elect, by a unanimous vote, a Superintendent for one year only. This was a move backward, and plainly in opposition to the better tendencies of our municipal life. An uncertain tenure will either divert or paralyze administrative energy. The man who is fit to be elected at all to a subordinate executive office, is fit to stay

---

[1] An oft-mooted point in the administration of the schools of the district is the extent to which classical instruction should be contained in the curriculum of the High School. The question is not a new one. The school included a Preparatory Collegiate Department from 1859 to 1867. The onslaught upon the school in 1866 led to the abolition of the Preparatory Department, but that course was re-introduced in September, 1877. Again, from year to year, the argument gathers force that the community should not pay for the special education of a few.

elected.   A faithful Superintendent could work untrammeled,
if he were chosen either for six years or during good behavior,
subject to removal, under a long notice, by a two-thirds vote
of the board.

THE TOWN GOVERNMENT.

The government of the town of New Haven is the parent
trunk upon which all the other local organizations have
grown.   Every year the electors of New Haven choose
incumbents for the time-honored offices of sealers, assessors,
pound-keepers, haywards, grand jurors, constables, surveyors
of highways, fence-viewers, gaugers and inspectors, packers,
weighers, justices of the peace, selectmen, members of board
of relief, managers of town deposit fund, registrars of voters,
auditors, a town clerk, tax collector, treasurer, town agent,
and registrar of vital statistics.   These officers, numbering in
all 151, rule a town three-fourths of whose territory are
within city limits.   Their authority extends over city and
country alike unless, in the former case, the city charter has
provided other channels of administration.   Apart from the
officers connected with the Treasury and Tax Department,
the most important town trusts are those of the selectmen and
town agent.

The powers of these and the other functionaries are, in
general, such as are customarily possessed by town officers.
But the existence of the city intensifies the responsibilities of
the selectmen, and the town agent holds what politicians
consider a strategic position.   The town agent is the financial
representative of the board of selectmen, and, as such, practically controls the distribution of "Outdoor Relief."   His
tenure of office by popular choice is not strictly according to
law, which supposes him to be elected by his colleagues upon
the board.   So long as the selectmen acquiesce in the selection made by people at the polls, there will be no trouble,
but, should the board ever reject the officer so selected, there
would be an unpleasant collision between law and custom.

Furthermore, the town agent, who holds his office by reason of an election in Town-Meeting, is virtually, if not legally, responsible directly to the voters in Town-Meeting assembled. Such a responsibility might work no ill in a quiet country town, but a town which contains a city is in different circumstances. A Town-Meeting of two hundred voters will know how such a trust is administered ; a Town-Meeting of thirteen thousand voters will never know.

It is not intended to imply that the town agency in New Haven has been mismanaged. Under existing circumstances it is almost inevitable that some duties of the office should be shirked, but, for the present, it is sufficient to assert that the principle rather than the practice is at fault. When the town agent was appointed by the selectmen as a body, and was plainly accountable to them, he was under the control of men necessarily familiar with the business of his office, and able to remove him if he should be incompetent or unsatisfactory. In case of a dispute between the majority of the board and a town agent, the latter can now assert against his colleagues the authority of a separate mandate from the people. Such an argument might be made both powerful and pernicious. There is a principle of government which must, sooner or later, win acceptance — viz.: "Subordinate administrative officers should be appointed, not elected." The town agent is, by the nature of his duties, subordinate to the selectmen, and no worthy reason demands his elevation. The town agent himself does not touch a cent of the money that is distributed. To every applicant he can give no more than an order upon the town treasury. This is better than the arrangement in some of our cities, where the town agent hands the money directly to the one who seeks relief. Hartford publishes annually a list of the names of those who have obtained money from the town agent, and the sum paid is placed opposite to each name. Such a detailed publication is so eminently proper and useful that no false sentiment should prevent the adoption of the custom by the town of New Haven in its town agent's report.

The Town-Meeting.

The ultimate fact in the town government is the annual Town-Meeting, the ancient General Court for the town, the folk-moot of all the voters resident in the Republic of New Haven. At one time it elects the town's officers; and, at another day, as a business-meeting, it hears the reports of the town's overseers, it authorizes or sanctions expenditures, it reviews the estimates of proportion, and determines the annual town-tax for seventy-five thousand people. Besides the dignity with which it is endowed by actual service, it is ennobled by the glory of antiquity and by the charm of historic associations. This most venerable institution in the community appears to-day in the guise of a gathering of a few citizens who do the work of as many thousands. The few individuals who are or have been officially interested in the government of the town meet together, talk over matters in a friendly way, decide what the rate of taxation for the coming year shall be, and adjourn. If others are present, it is generally as spectators rather than as participants. Only the few understand the subjects which are under discussion. Even if Demos should be present in greater force, he would almost inevitably obey the voice of some well-informed and influential member of the town government of his own party. But citizens of all parties and of all shades of respectability ignore the Town-Meeting and School-Meeting alike. Not one-seventieth part of the citizens of the town has attended an annual Town-Meeting; they hardly know when it is held.

The newspapers give its transactions a scant notice, which some of their subscribers probably read. The actual governing force of the town is, therefore, an oligarchy in the bosom of a slumbering democracy. But the town is well governed. The town government carries too little spoil to attract those unreliable politicians who infest the City Council. If the ruling junta should venture upon too lavish a use of the town's money, an irresistible check would appear at once.

Any twenty citizens could force the selectmen to summon the town together, and the apparent oligarchy would doubtless go down before the awakened people. The possibility of such a folk-moot will be sufficient to avert from school district and town the danger of dishonesty, if not of unwisdom.

CONSOLIDATION.

The proposal to abolish the dual system of town and city government, and to substitute in its place a single administration for the whole territory, is now becoming familiar to every one. Several other cities in New England have the same combination of jurisdictions, and the same problem has been discussed there also.

Agitation of the subject in New Haven circles dates as far back as 1852. The abortive attempt at that period has been already noticed. The good feeling between town and city was not then disturbed, and the first sign of a rupture did not appear until June, 1865, when a Town-Meeting expressed strong resentment against recent action by the city government. A protest was placed upon the records against objectionable amendments to the city charter, then pending in the Legislature, which threatened to augment the power of the city at the undue expense of the town. In 1870, the greater part of the eastern portion of the township was subjected to the city government, but, eleven years later, the loss was replaced by the union with the town of the western and more important half of the town of East Haven, including the borough of Fair Haven and all the lands bordering the eastern side of New Haven harbor. The consent of the inhabitants of that district and of East Haven Town could be gained for the annexation only under the condition that the junction should be with the town, and not with the city. No little opposition has been excited, therefore, by petitions from

the city to the Legislature in 1883, and again in 1884 and
1885, to secure " The consolidation of the governments of
the City of New Haven, the Town of New Haven, and the
Borough of Fair Haven East."

The ordinary city-voter probably deems it to be plainly
absurd that he should help to support two separate governments in one community. It seems reasonable to him that one
set of officers should do all the public business. In the majority
of the one hundred and fifty-two offices on the town ticket the
average voter has but little interest. In the party conven-
tions the Board of Selectmen and the Board of Relief are
partitioned in the ratios of four to three and three to two,
usually in favor of the Democrats, without expectation of a
contest. The auditorships, and the registrarships of voters
are evenly divided between the parties. For the remaining
town-offices, one hundred and thirty-eight in all, each political
camp presents its candidates, indeed, but neither convention
cares to remain in session for their nomination. Each convention delegates the selection of the host of sealers, weighers,
viewers, etc., to its chairman, or to a committee, and ad-
journs. Then a few gentlemen meet around a table and
arrange the rest of the ticket as seemeth best to them. The
citizen possibly learns the names of his party's candidates
upon the town-ticket by a hasty glance at the morning paper,
or at the printed slip which is given him at the polls. Thus
the composition of the town's government for another year is
determined.

Under these circumstances there is nothing surprising in
the impression that the town-government is a luxury rather
than a necessity. It has been contended, therefore, that the
interests of economy, and prompt, impartial administration,
demand the rule of the whole township by one government—
that the city-government should be the one preserved ; and
that the burdens of taxation in the outlying township could
be made commensurate with the privileges enjoyed. It is
complained that the proceeds of town-taxes, which come chiefly

from the pockets of the city, are expended mainly upon the
outlying portions of the township.   Over the conduct of that
expenditure the city-government has no control.   It is asserted
that the city's money ought to be used in the improvement of
the streets of the city rather than of the suburbs.   Another
assertion is that the care of the poor is too important a trust
to be administered by the town-agent and selectmen.   The
independent jurisdiction of the Town-Meeting is the greatest
stumbling-block, and it is claimed that, since a common power
succeeds in collecting town and city taxes, a common power
might also manage the imposition of taxes.   Mayor Lewis
declares, "The plan of laying taxes and making appropriations in Town-Meetings like ours has never, since the Dark
Ages, been tried by any community of 75,000 inhabitants.
Boston discarded it when she numbered but little more than
40,000, and when her taxes were but little more than half
what our Town-Meeting now annually votes."

To this presentation of the case there are weighty objections
and eager objectors.   So long as any part of the township
remains outside the city-limits, the whole town-organization
is essential, and if either government is abolished, the city
must be merged in the town.   There are constitutional
reasons why town-officers must be retained.

Article V, Section 5, of the State Constitution reads:
"The Selectmen and Town-Clerk of the several towns shall
decide on the qualifications of electors at such times and in
such manner as may be prescribed by law."

Also Article X, Section 2: "Each town shall annually
elect Selectmen, and such officers of local police as the laws
may prescribe."

These obstacles are small in size, but great in authority.
The town-government cannot be directly abolished.   If the
city-limits should be extended so that the territory of town
and city should be everywhere co-extensive and coterminous,
and so that the town-boundaries should become also the city-
boundaries, it is evident that the one city-government would

practically enjoy single sway; but it will be a long time before
the city can thus grow apace. About one-quarter of the
township and about one-eighteenth of its population now lie
outside the city. Against every proposal to extend the city
it is, and will be, urged that a large proportion of this outlying territory is farming land, unfit for share in urban
police, fire, gas, and street privileges, and unable to bear the
burden of urban taxation.

There would always be a tendency on the part of the city
to tax the suburban districts as heavily as possible, and
rascally politicians would discover a fine quarry for jobs in
new portions of the city. It is asserted that no adjustment
of the city-taxation is possible which would not make the
rates upon farm-lands higher than at present, without con-
ferring a single benefit in return. There is already some
farm-land within the city, but the border districts of the city
bear, with the central portions of the same, the uniform rate
of $19\frac{1}{2}$ mills. If a large outlying tract were united with the
city on condition of taxation proportional to benefits, some
considerable part of the present city might reasonably call
out for justice. The city of Burlington, Vt., includes some
agricultural territory, and the assessors, in making up the
grand list, reckon the farms at a figure which prevents
excessive taxation. But the population and territory of New
Haven Town and City differ much in quantity, quality, and
situation from those of Burlington.

The certainty of a tempered breeze upon the shorn lamb
would be much less assured in New Haven, and, indeed, the
feasibility of proper "tempering" would be less practicable.
Only about six hundred people dwell upon the farm-districts
of Burlington, and it seems improbable that the compact
portion of the city will seek extension in their direction.

It will be seen that neither party pleads without a reason.
The city is the taxpayer of the town, and has a right to
demand economy. The town-government, on the other
hand, is rooted in the fundamental law of the State, and,

while it exists as at present, it averts even the danger of undue taxation from suburban districts. Two principles which seem to me almost axiomatic would, if properly heeded, settle the dispute.

1. No city should extend farther than it is built up.

2. A city needs room for growth. Remembering that a city exists for business purposes, there can be no good reason for even pretending to put policemen, pavements, and gas mains in the middle of a sand-plain. When the outlying districts are crowded with inhabitants, the people will, of themselves, demand admission to city-privileges.

Secondly, there can be no more favorable conditions for expansion than where a parent town is the rind covering and surrounding the city at the core. The city can then spread out its skirts without infringing upon the rights of another town. Every dollar which the city-taxpayer expends for the improvement of the outlying township helps to ensure the growth of the city and of its traffic, and the contentment of its inhabitants.

No city can exist without a suburban belt of partly rural dwellers who live by means of the city, but are unable to shoulder its burdens. If the city reaches out to include this belt, no amount of adjustment will prevent the formation of a new girdle outside the new boundaries. At present, the most practicable improvement seems to me to be a consolidation of functions, rather than of jurisdictions. So far as possible, the same man should hold the similar offices of both town and city. The principal objection to the existing Town-Meeting might be obviated if the care of the poor, of roads and bridges, was entrusted to municipal boards, subject, indeed, to the mayor, but containing elected representatives of the suburban districts. The expenditures of such departments could, by the aid of the grand list, be apportioned between city and suburbs. Alterations of such a nature might possibly produce satisfactory results, always providing that the outlying township, so long as it remained rural, should not be subjected to

the City Council. The structure of the city-government is
not yet so sound that a suburban population would care for
shelter under it at the price of additional mills on the dollar.

THE CITY-GOVERNMENT.

There is an historic propriety, if no other, in choosing town-
officers upon party-tickets, for the town is a miniature republic,
a mirror of the State, a State-atom. But the city is an
economic, and not a political unit. It is a business corporation, endowed for business purposes, and it bears the least
intrinsic resemblance to the ancient city, which was, indeed,
a State. When the true essence and meaning of the modern
city shall be generally comprehended, there will be a wondrous
reformation in city-administrations. A mayor will then be
chosen as a railway corporation chooses its superintendent—
for good character and business ability—and there will be no
more attention paid to his views about the tariff, or States'
rights, than to his opinions concerning predestination and
original sin. But, like most of our cities, New Haven has
been governed, since Jackson's day, with prime reference to
political partisanship. Here and there a member of the city-
government commands more than a party-fealty, and is
universally recognized as deserving office by reason of ability
and integrity. But, in general, the voters of the city hear
and obey the party-whip in matters purely municipal, and
offices are shared at each election with every reference to
long purses, to popularity with the "Boys," to the claims of
clique and party service. The partisan qualification is
deemed as necessary in one camp as in the other.

The city is gradually advancing upon the same road over
which its neighbors, New York and Brooklyn, have already
traveled. Saloons are becoming the seed-beds of official
enterprise, and the whiskey-vendor is a growing factor in
political calculations. For some time the machine of the
corrupt, selfish, and irresponsible "Boss" has been grinding

effectually.   The factors of the problem, both for him and for ourselves, must be clearly apprehended.

First, what may be expected of the voters?

The dominant elements furnish many obstacles to any scheme for better government that includes universal suffrage. Criticism must be based, to a certain extent, on the supposition that the popular majority can be depended upon to choose good rather than evil.   But the ideal municipal structure, if it could be erected to-day in New Haven, would, unquestionably, soon be wrenched out of shape, because it must perforce rest upon some foundation of ignorance and foolish partisan prejudice.   It is equally true that the intents and motives of the mass of the people are good and true, and worthy, in the long run, of confident trust.   Sooner or later, honest men, without regard to party, profession, birth, or education, stand together and strike the evil down.   But, until the moment of righteous indignation comes, the demagogues and selfseekers of either party are likely to muster the most voters.   How shall the city live during the intervals when the public conscience is inactive?

Is it better to attempt continuous regulation by a system of checks, divided powers and responsibilities, and external interferences, or to give each sphere of government its normal freedom of action, leaving to the people the responsibility of approval and condemnation?   It seems to me that the latter course is the wiser.   The reasonable safeguards of public inspection and of minority representation need not be discarded, but, in general, every legislative or executive organ of government should have an undivided allegiance, simple functions, and should be within easy reach of the freemen at the polls. The verdict of the people, tardy, ill-formed, and unjust as it may be, is properly conclusive in all our legislation and administration.   However disappointing the actual daily conditions and results of popular election may prove to be, it is certain that every political act, be it good or ill in itself, contributes unceasingly to the popular education, and the trend of popular education is, as yet, upward, not downward. Public opinion can be conquered by public opinion. Every allowance being made for the difficulties that will inevitably retard the realization of theory, the principal problem of our municipal life is ready for analysis.

The City Judiciary.

At the outset it appears that the city government is patterned closely upon the old English plan, and bears, with its legislative charter, executive head, bicameral council, and separate judiciary, the usual resemblance to the American type of government, whether national, provincial, or local. But here at once the observer stumbles upon a relic of ancient usage in the practical separation of the city judiciary from the electors of the locality. Constables, justices of the peace, and a sheriff are elected by the citizens, but the city courts derive existence directly from the Legislature. From the beginning the State Legislature has been a prominent agent in New Haven's history. The retention of power over the judiciary is a part of the same jealousy of civic action that caused the Legislature to hold the mayor in office at its own pleasure until 1826, and to elect probate judges until 1851. There is no longer any fear that city officers will set up monarchical forms of government and subvert the liberties of the State, but the power of the Legislature over the City Court is now exerted in order that the Republican party of the city may find more ample representation in its government. The mode of selecting judges for New Haven is this: the New Haven County delegation to the dominant party in the Legislature assembles in caucus and nominates two of the same political faith to be, respectively, judge and assistant judge of the New Haven City Court. Their choice is adopted by their party, and the nominations are duly ratified, often by a strict party vote. Inasmuch as the Legislature is usually Republican and the city of New Haven is unfailingly Democratic, these usages amount to a reservation of judicial offices from the "hungry and thirsty" local majority, and the maintenance of a certain control by the Republican country towns over the Democratic city. During the present session of the Legislature (March, 1885) this argument was put forward in answer to a Democratic plea for representation upon the City Court Bench: "The Democrats possess all the other offices in New Haven. It's only fair that the Republicans should have the City Court." Each party accepted the statement as a conclusive reason for political action.

It would be gratifying to find the subject discussed upon a higher plane, and the incumbents of the offices who had done well continued from term to term without regard to party affiliations. But, in the present condition of political morals, the existing arrangements are probably the most practicable that could be made. It goes without saying that country districts are, as a rule, more deserving of political power than are cities. The method of selecting the judiciary is everywhere a mooted question, but it seems to me that the State authority should designate every judge of a rank higher than justice of the peace. If the city judges were locally elected upon the general party ticket, the successful candidates would often be under obligations to elements in the community who are the chief source and cause of the criminal class — an unseemly position for a judge.

The civil jurisdiction of the City Court includes all causes, both at law and in equity, whereto any of the parties reside in said city, except suits affecting land outside the city. When the value involved exceeds $100, a defendant residing outside the city may appeal to higher courts, and when the value involved exceeds $500, an appeal may be taken by any of the parties. The City Court has jurisdiction of all cases of summary process within the city, and the power to issue search-warrants. Its terms begin on the first Monday of each month. The regular sessions continue through the next two days, and include also the last week-day of each month.

The criminal jurisdiction of the court maintains, within the town of New Haven, the same powers which justices of the peace usually possess ; it includes the cognizance of crimes whose penalties do not exceed a two-hundred-dollar fine, or six months' imprisonment, or both.   Appeals may be allowed except upon convictions for drunkenness, profane cursing, and Sabbath-breaking.   Daily sessions are held on week-days, and on Sundays if the city attorney requests it.   The salaries of the two judges are $1,500 and $900 respectively, but in addition there are fees for each of $5 per day for each day of the civil session, and also of $2 for every hearing upon complaint for a commitment to the Connecticut Industrial School for Girls.   The judge has the sole right of appointing a city attorney at a salary of $2,500, and an assistant city attorney at a salary of $900 is appointed by the city attorney, subject to the approval of the judge.   The judge also appoints a clerk of the court and an assistant clerk at salaries of $1,000 and $200 per annum respectively.   Both the clerk and the attorney are further provided for by fees. Therefore, the judge controls, directly or indirectly, all appointments in his court, his own assistant alone excepted, involving salaries aggregating $4,600 aside from fees.

To sum up, the city judiciary is amenable to the State Legislature, and has no legal responsibility to the people of New Haven, who are represented in it only by the sheriff and by jurymen.   The court has both civil and criminal jurisdiction, subject to appeals to the County and Superior Courts.   The two judges are selected in a party caucus, and are generally local politicians, but the character of the bench has been good notwithstanding.   The chief judge wields practically all the patronage of the court.   The salaries to different officers of the court amount to $7,000, any or all of which may be raised, but not diminished, by the City Council.[1]

---

[1] The receipts of the court in fines and costs are less than they were formerly.   In 1875, the total amount of cash received was $18,633.04, of which the city treasury obtained $10,768.60.   In 1884, the estimated income from the City Court was $5,000.

THE CITY EXECUTIVE.

The structure of the city judiciary is clearly defined and simply planned. Defects in its operation can be easily traced to the culpable officer. But the city executive possesses no such merits. As a separate department it can hardly be said to exist. The Court of Common Council is the supreme authority in the city government. Some of the most important executive branches depend upon it, and owe no responsibility to the mayor. There exists, consequently, a variety of accountabilities.

The commissioners of public works, of police, and of fire, are the choice of the aldermen alone. The boards of compensation, the various scalers, supervisors, and inspectors, result from the joint action of the City Council. The commissioners of public buildings and of public health are the creatures, officially, of the mayor plus the consenting aldermen. The coroner acknowledges a similar genesis, the Court of Common Council being substituted in the place of the aldermen. The Park Commission is produced by the most intricate process of all.

Two of them are chosen in the same manner as the commissioners of public buildings and public health. Three are first elected by citizen donors to the East Rock Park, the votes being cast in proportion to the amount contributed, on a basis of one vote for every gift of $100 in money or two acres of land. The elections must be ratified by the mayor. These three citizen commissioners form a close corporation, electing their own successors, but always subject to the approval of the mayor. Furthermore, the mayor may remove any such citizen commissioner for cause, and, in case of failure to elect a successor, he may appoint to the vacancy. Moreover, several executive officers who are elected by the whole town, such as the tax collector and the Board of Education, have unabridged authority throughout the city. Finally the city elects at large a sheriff and a mayor. Here are seven different sources of executive power, and four of them are double. Only the mayor and sheriff in the city executive are directly responsible to the people. The most vital parts of the administration feel the sway of the City Council only.

The city government is emphatically a government of commissions. This will be apparent when the actual functions of the mayoralty are examined. The mayor serves the city for two years at a salary of $3,000 per annum. The great majority of the list of powers expressly delegated to him by charter are those of a conservator of the peace. He is the chief sheriff, and reaches the height of his powers when, under great stress, he makes requisition for the militia of the city. His appointing power, as we have already seen, is limited, and is practically absolute only in respect to the citizen park commissioners, but even then only under certain conditions. .

As chairman of the different boards, the mayor wields a more direct influence upon the governmental action. He can preside, with a casting vote, in the Board of Aldermen, and likewise in the joint convention of the Common Council, which can be called in case the separate boards fail to make the necessary elections. He has merely a delaying veto, the majority vote in each board being sufficient to overrule his objection. The mayor is also *ex-officio* member and chairman of the Board of Public Health, with only the casting vote. He is *ex-officio* member and chairman of the Boards of Public Works, of Fire, and of Police, but is deprived of his usual casting vote when the question concerns the selection of voting-places in the city or town, by the police commissioners, and the election or dismissal of any employee by any of the boards. The mayor is also an active member of the Park Commission.

Finally, the mayor exerts his greatest actual power in the department of finance. He is an active member and a presiding officer of the Board of Finance, which is one of the

most important wheels in the city machinery. Here the
mayor may make himself really felt in determining the
amount of appropriations and loans, the rate of taxation, in
examining accounts of officers, in allowing and counter-
signing tax liens, claims, and orders.

Thus it seems that the mayor's chief duties which afford
employment are his very limited appointing power, and his
oversight and share of the management of the city's financial
affairs. His legal inability to dissolve a tie in the commissions over a proposed election or dismissal directly removes
from him responsibility for the conduct of the various
departments, and constitutes a readiness to read the Riot Act
under possible provocation his chief personal obligation.
By virtue of the mayor's power as guardian of the public
peace he is vested, through the city's ordinances, with a number of police duties of a minor sort. He may restrict the use
of steam whistles, offer rewards for the arrest of criminals,
give advice to subordinate officers, designate horse-car stands,
and recommend licenses to venders, but, in the majority of
such functions, the assent of the aldermen is requisite. The
aldermen, indeed, are empowered to override the mayor's
possible refusal to allow the city clerk to license a street
peddler. Thus it will be seen that New Haven has not as yet
adopted the modern theory of centralizing all the executive
powers and obligations upon one single head. When compared with a city like Brooklyn, whose mayor is a despot,
and, on the other hand, with one like San Francisco, whose
mayor is largely ornamental, New Haven resembles the
latter rather than the former. At any rate, it is on the San
Francisco side of a middle line.

THE CITY LEGISLATURE.

The mainspring of the urban administration is not in the
mayoralty. We must search for it elsewhere. Only through
the consultative and legislative machinery of the City Council

some of the most important executive powers are made practically operative. Omitting reference to the sheriff, a judicial
rather than an executive officer, and deferring consideration
of all commissions for the present, we are confronted first by
the question, "How was the existing equilibrium, or lack
thereof, attained?"

The present position of New Haven's Court of Common
Council is the reasonable result of the municipal development of a century. History has already shown the extreme
caution with which the freemen of the city have bestowed
enlarged powers upon any authority not wholly their own
representative. It has been observed how, at every turn,
quick jealousy, both in State and city, hedged in the monarchical mayoralty. Consent of the freemen themselves, in City-
Meeting assembled, was necessary to ratify actions of the
mayor and Council. Not until 1854 was a remedy sought
for this state of things. When the City-Meeting disappeared,
the mantle of its supremacy naturally fell upon its nearest
representative, the City Council, composed of delegates of the
people. So, when the increase of wealth and numbers necessitated an expansion of the administration, and a new
co-ordination of departments, the Council was consistently
endowed with full control, and with the originating authority.

The twelve wards of the city choose sixty men, of whom
thirty-six are called "Councilmen," and twenty-four, "Aldermen." These two boards together form the Court of Common
Council. Of each board the presidents of the Police, Public
Works, Public Health, and Fire Commissions are *ex-officio*
members, with every right except that of voting. By city
ordinance the aldermen meet regularly on the first Monday
of every month, and the councilmen on the second Monday;
but the mayor may convene them whenever he deems it
expedient. Each board elects a president, and the president
of the Board of Aldermen is the vice-mayor of the city.
The city clerk is the clerk of the same board. In either
branch a majority is a quorum. Attendance may be made

compulsory, upon warrant issued by the mayor or president
to the sheriff of the county or the city, whenever such warrant
is requested by the members of the board in attendance.   No
measure can be put to final vote in one board on the same
day when it passed the other, except by unanimous consent.
A proposed enactment may be referred to the suitable commissioners as though they were a standing committee, and a
majority vote can pass ordinances over the mayor's veto.
Elections within the council must be by ballot.   Presiding
officers of the council, or of its committees, are competent to
compel witnesses to attend and testify.   The Board of Aldermen has standing committees upon buildings, lamps, licenses,
and numbering streets.   There are joint standing committees
of the Common Council upon appropriations, auditing, building lines, claims, the fire department, nominations, ordinances,
printing, railroads and bridges, sewers, streets, squares, and
water.   The Common Council, by ordinance, may also
appoint a committee to manage any sinking fund that may be
established, and a joint committee of assessment, which per-
forms the functions of a Board of Compensation.   The
charter provides that no vote, unless by unanimous consent,
shall be taken in either branch upon a measure that has not
been examined and reported upon by the proper committee
or Board of Commissioners.

The Common Council alone controls the finances and can
borrow money.   It can appropriate funds, and order taxation,
and the charter places some checks upon this right.   Not
more than six thousand dollars can be devoted yearly to the
necessities of the Park, and fifteen hundred dollars is the
limit put upon expenditure for any public celebration.
Most important of all is the provision that no appropriation
for any object shall exceed the estimate by more than one
hundred dollars, unless by a vote of five-sixths of each board.
Publication of the proceedings and votes can be insured by
any member of the court.   The principal joint committee is
the Board of Finance, chosen by the Common Council from
among its own members, and comprising also the mayor.

The mode of determining taxation is substantially as follows. In November of each year the Board of Finance prepares an estimate of the necessary expenditure of the city for the year ensuing, of its liabilities and resources, and of the necessary rate of taxation. The calculated expenditure must be specific, classified under the proper heads and departments. The report forthwith is submitted to the Common, Council and published in the newspapers. Before the first of January, the Common Council shall have revised the estimates, levied taxes upon the last completed grand list of the town, and shall have specified all the items of appropriation. The charter forbids that the total annual appropriation shall exceed the estimated income for that year, and that any officer shall make any payment or incur any liability in excess of the amount appropriated by the council to any object. All special taxes must be laid in a similar manner. Whenever a tax has been duly laid the proper rate-bill is prepared and signed by a committee of four aldermen, with the mayor, and then delivered, with a warrant for the collection of the specified tax, to the collector of the city. The charter, which generally sins by omission rather than by commission, nowhere gives the mayor the right to veto parts of appropriation bills, and there is no clause limiting the possible indebtedness of the city. The tax for city expenses alone is now about nine dollars *per capita*, or eleven dollars on the thousand. This rate is probably nearly double the actual cost on the thousand upon a full valuation in either New York or Philadelphia.

Legislative Control over the Commissions.

Turning now to the confirming and appointing powers of the Common Council, we shall discover the legislative branch trenching upon the proper prerogatives of the executive, and granting to its own creatures the usage of the moneys which itself has appropriated by taxation. The old style of city government, which was modeled upon the ancient pattern of the London municipality, accorded to the unpaid committees of the City Council the executive disposition of the sums which the whole council had appropriated. In other words, " The individual members spent the money which the whole body voted." New Haven's present plan offers these three variations from the usual custom : The aldermen alone choose the Commissions of Public Works, Police, and Fire; with the exception of the mayor, as hereinbefore stated, no member of the city government is eligible; and it is intended that the commissions shall be non-partisan. There are six members of each commission, who serve for three years. Two commissioners for each board are annually chosen in January. The provision for securing non-partisan commissions is that each alderman shall have but one vote, and that the two persons receiving the highest equal or unequal numbers of ballots shall be declared elected. Ordinarily, this must secure a commission evenly balanced between the two parties.

Further restrictions upon membership are : 1. That no one shall be a member of more than one commission at the same time; 2. That no member shall enter into any contract to do work for the city; 3. That no member shall receive any employment under the commissions; and 4. That no police commissioner shall be engaged as principal, agent, or employee in the manufacture or sale of intoxicating liquors. If a vacancy occurs, the charter provides that only a member of the same political party as the outgoing commissioner shall be eligible to succeed him. The Commission of Public Works is forbidden to begin any operation other than ordinary repairs until the task has been authorized by vote of the Common Council. Such is the genesis of these three commissions, which demand a high degree of executive ability on the part of their officers, which form the bulk of the municipal administration, and which absorb two-thirds of the total annual expenditure. The actual expenditure of these departments in 1883 and the estimated expense of the same for 1884 are thus compared:

	1883.	1884.
Public Works, . .	$199,344.71	$233,735.00
Police, ...	108,400.00	106,325.00
Fire, ...	82,275.00	80,925.00
Health, ...	6,300.00	7,400.00
	————$396,319.71	———— $428,385.00
Harbor Department, . .	250.00	200.00
Sundries, ...	218,313.00	224,880.00
Total of City, . . .	$614,882.71	$653,465.00

Without reckoning the wages paid to ordinary labor, and without reckoning fees, a little more than two hundred thousand dollars is annually paid by the city in salaries. Of this sum fourteen thousand and seven hundred dollars are paid in accordance with charter stipulations, and to officers chosen outside of the Common Council, excepting in the latter respect the corporation counsel and the assistant city clerk. The residue is disposed of directly by vote of the Common Council, or of one of the four commissions. In the item of salaries there might profitably be some retrenchment, and the charter itself creates the most expensive sinecure in the city government. The corporation counsel receives five hundred dollars a year more than the mayor obtains, but does very little to earn his wage. A better economy would direct the city to consult an ordinary lawyer and pay the fee on the few occasions when a legal opinion is needed. The city ought not to maintain a prize for the New Haven Bar Association.

Finally, the confirming power of the council together, or of the aldermen alone, is, of course, confined to those few officials who are subject to the mayor's nomination, the coroner, the three commissioners of public buildings, the six commissioners of public health, and two park commissioners. These commissions, however important in duties, are comparatively weak in authority. The park commissioners are limited to a six-thousand-dollar appropriation for the East Rock Park. The thirteen other inclosures in different parts of the city are cared for by the Board of Public Works.

The commissioners of public buildings can only submit

recommendations to the Board of Aldermen. All the afore-
said appointees combined do not control appropriations of
more than fifteen thousand dollars. The restrictions upon
membership in these commissions are, in general, similar to
those previously described. All the commissions are unpaid,
but these last-named differ from the former in that there is
no endeavor to render them non-partisan.

Excluding the Park Commission, which is entirely unique
in structure, all the city commissions enjoy yet another
common feature. Removal of any commissioner is at the
discretion of the Board of Aldermen alone. Although the
mayor nominates seventeen different commissioners, the only
officers in the whole city government who are in this way
amenable to him are, in the first place, as it seems, a coroner,
and secondly, three park commissioners, whom, in all proba-
bility, he did not nominate, and whom he may only con-
ditionally remove. The charter-law regulating removals and
tenure of office is that city officers chosen by electors shall
hold office through their term, or until a successor is chosen
and sworn, but that in case of resignation, death, removal, or
incapacity of an officer, the Court of Common Council shall
order a special election.

A subsequent section provides that all persons holding any
office created by law by virtue of an election or appointment,
may be removed by the body having the power to appoint
them. In general, "Appointees and employees shall be
removable at the pleasure of the person or body having the
right to employ or appoint them."[1] But, in order to preclude
the possibility of a dispute between the appointing power of
the mayor and the confirming power of the aldermen, the
responsibility of the five commissions was thus asserted :

"Any member of said boards shall be subject to removal
by the Board of Aldermen for cause, upon charges made in
writing by any member of either Board of the Court of Common Council, provided said charges are found to be sustained

[1] Sections 17 and 58.

by a two-thirds vote of the Board of Aldermen."[1] The numerous public servants who are, or may be, elected by the Court of Common Council, acting conjointly, play for the most part a minor *rôle* in the municipal economy.[2]

No matter what laws and theories may affirm, the body which elects and removes is the dominant authority. Therefore it is fair to say that the city executive owes directly a divided allegiance—the mayor to the people, but the commissions to the Common Council first of all. In the Common Council the Board of Aldermen obtains the lion's share, and thus practically becomes the truest centre of the municipal activity in all branches except the judicial. In other words, the law-making, tax-laying power can dictate not only *how* money shall be spent, but also *who* shall spend it. If the executive departments of the National Government were managed by commissions of six men each, elected by the Senate, or by the House of Representatives, or both, without the possibility of any interference by the President, the state of affairs would be outwardly parallel. The idea suggests such possibilities of non-performance of duty, of political engineering and scandal, of the most nebulous of Star Routes, that the explanation of the common degeneracy of cities under our forms of government seems to leap to the surface.

The commission appointed by Governor Hartranft, of Pennsylvania, to study the problems of municipal govern-

---

[1] Section 36, *ad finem.*

[2] The number of town-officers elected by ballot, including the Board of Education, reaches one hundred and sixty. The city government contains two hundred and fifty-two individuals who annually draw a stated salary, but only sixty-five of the city's officials are chosen directly by popular suffrage. Therefore four hundred and twelve persons perform the more prominent functions of municipal life in school-district, town, and city. Two hundred and twenty-five of them are elected by the people. An estimate of the entire number of men employed in any capacity, principal or subordinate, occasionally or continuously, in the local public service, places the sum at twelve hundred. About one in every fifty-eight of the people of New Haven is guarding the common interests of the municipal bodies politic, and is encamped upon the common pocket-book.

ment in that State reported in 1877 as follows : " The heads
of departments appointed by the councils are merely the
agents of committees, not only in the administration of trusts
supposed to be committed to departments, and in the appointment of subordinate officers, but in the payment of bills and
current expenses not embraced in special contracts, thus
affording opportunity for, if not inviting, corrupt combina-
tions between the two branches of the city government.
This condition of things exists only in city governments, and
is found neither in State nor Nation." New Haven cannot
be classed with the cities that are discussed in this report.
There has been no scandalous misuse of the public funds,
and the commissions are not quite the same as committees of
the council. There is, however, one exception to the general
authority of the commissions. The street-lamps of the city
have never been placed under the care of the Public Works'
Department, but are under the sole supervision of an aldermanic standing committee. This committee manages the
entire lamp account, and chooses the lamp inspector. No
valid reason appears for the retention of the old usage in
this single instance. It seems to be merely a sop thrown to
the Board of Aldermen.

Conduct of Commissions.

The political equilibrium maintained in the commissions
supplies a check upon some kinds of possible misconduct.
But the evils appertaining to the system have been pushed
beneath the surface, not eradicated. The probe of examination reveals the confusion that attends an intermingling of
responsibilities.

Of course King Caucus rules ; the Democratic aldermen
determining one-half the membership of the Public Works,
Fire, and Police Commissions, the Republican members
naming as absolutely the other half. The history of the Police
Commission during the winter of 1885 is one of the best

practical commentaries that can be offered upon the whole system. Near the beginning of the year the chief of police was removed by death.

This is the most important office within the gift of the police commissioners, both · by reason of the salary and of the influence involved. It is the chief of police who, among other duties, issues licenses for billiard tables, bowling alleys, public exhibitions, and public conveyances, and who receives information from his force of all violations of city laws and ordinances. These facts, added to a realizing sense of· the activity which an energetic and right-minded chief can impart to the police force in general, stimulate the liquor-selling and drinking interests of the city to take a vigorous interest in the choice of this officer. Therefore it was not surprising that when the half-dozen commissioners met for election, the three Democrats and the three Republicans were found to entertain totally diverse ideals of the coming incumbent.

The commission first assembled to fill the vacancy January 8th, 1885. The remarks of Democratic Commissioner Catlin, himself his party's nominee for the chieftainship, struck the key-note of the struggle as it seemed to him and to his friends. He said that the "Board [*sc.* of Commissioners], as constituted, consisted of three Democrats and three Republicans. The officers of the force stood about 8 to 3. Elect a Republican for chief, and the force would have a preponderance of Republicans among its head officers."[1] He could not, therefore, vote for a Republican candidate, and he hoped that the Republicans would see things as he did. Republican Commissioner Sheldon contended that politics had nothing to do with the matter.

Mr. Catlin replied that he desired fairness. "He thought that as good a man could be got on the Democratic side as on the Republican."

After this explanation of the prime motives for the bestowal

---

[1] Report in *Journal and Courier*, January 9th.

of municipal responsibilities the voting began, and resulted
in a tie. There the question hung while the presiding
mayor looked helplessly on. Candidates were proposed who
would ensure a business-like, non-partisan, and law-supporting
administration of the police force, but no agreement was
reached, and there seemed to be some justification for the
advertising squib in the newspapers, "Wanted—a Chief of
Police for New Haven. Nobody who is fit for the place
need apply." During the deadlock, the terms of two commissioners ended, and the aldermen chose their successors,
but the contest remained unaltered. Meanwhile, the captain
of the police force was acting chief, and perhaps, if strict
ideas of Municipal-Service Reform could prevail, the captain
ought to stand in line of promotion to the permanent chieftainship.

Finally, during the third week in July, the prolonged
contest was ended. The commissioners were, in a sense,
compelled to elect a Democratic fellow-commissioner, who
was too good a man to be chosen in the first place. A few
days later the Democratic aldermen met to select a commissioner to succeed the new chief. They exemplified their
fitness to control the city executive by falling straightway
into a violent quarrel over the claims of German Democrats
to representation upon the commission. One City Father,
of Teutonic extraction, was enraged because he had been told
that no Dutchman could have the place, and that, if he
didn't like it, he could lump it. The supporters of the non-
German candidate, having the advantage of numbers, depre-
cated the raising of a race-issue. Upon such a plane an
important executive appointment was discussed, and made.

We can see now out of what material the aldermen con-
struct their commissions; and we can also see how the
present system lacks order, directness, and free motion. The
executive is hampered. The legislative branch does nothing
to clear away obstacles. So far as elections like the foregoing are concerned, the idea of non-partisanship in the
commissions becomes farcical.

Here is a so-called non-partisan commission which protracts a partisan deadlock through seven months. Yet, without the balance of parties in the commission, the state of affairs under the existing supremacy of the aldermen would be worse. The question reduces itself to a dilemma, illustrative of the disordered system of government: if the non-partisan boards are maintained, the administration is likely to be clogged, and there are unseemly disputes and delays; if the non-partisan feature is abandoned, and the present source of election retained, the administration is likely to fall into the hands of less competent, and possibly less honest, officers.

It must be conceded, moreover, that the determination of a so-called non-partisan board is, in very many cases, not the agreement of the board's united wisdom, but is the resultant compromise of the conflicting party interests that are represented in the board; it is apt to be a temporary makeshift, not a permanent solution. Non-partisan commissions are, in themselves, confessions that party government in cities is a failure, and that politics should be removed from municipal matters. These commissions seek to redeem the failure by balancing one party against another so evenly that neither of them can do anything without corrupting or overpowering the other. Is it thought that a dog does not chew his bone properly? Put three dogs at one end of the bone and three more at the other end; then the non-partisan commission will proceed at once to arrange matters. The method is clumsy, if not dangerous.

During the winter of 1885, a demonstration was made before the State Legislative Committee on cities and boroughs in favor of the election of non-partisan commissions on a general ticket by the voters at large, no elector being allowed to cast a ballot for more than half the membership of each commission. Some advantages appear in this plan. The commissions would directly represent the people, and the fatal entanglement with the City Council would be removed. But there are insurmountable objections. All co-ordination and dependence in the municipal executive would be destroyed, and the city would be provided with so many more mayors. "Subordinate administrative officers should be appointed, not elected."

Executive Organization.

The course of municipal development in our principal cities has been toward the consolidation of the Executive Department. New Haven, though a small city, has now in its charter the same provisions which proved disastrous to its larger neighbors, and which impelled them to recast their system of government. Their experience has emphasized the truth of this principle:

"The popular branch should tell *how* the money of the community shall be spent, but should not tell *who* shall superintend the spending." The officers of administration should be closely connected with the body of taxpayers— whose work those officers do—and not with a legislative body, which should be freed from every inducement to warp the laws for selfish purposes. System and uniform action in the administration can be secured only by the strong hand of a single superior.

The mayor, therefore, should appoint the heads of departments, and the mayor and his heads of departments should have the control of all their subordinates. The mayor is the servant and representative of the people, and he should be responsible to his employers for every branch of the municipal service, from city engineer to lamp cleaner. The people can fasten responsibility upon a mayor; it is difficult to trace it in a crowd of common councilmen. A representative body which wields executive power affords an inviting opportunity for log-rolling, dickering, and partisan management; at least some of its members are always comparatively unknown men, who can traffic in the public welfare under the shadow of obscurity. The mayor must act in the full light of public opinion. He is a character known and read of all men; if such an officer is allowed to pursue evil courses without hindrance, it must be because the majority of his constituency is no better than himself.

A mayor who is directly responsible for the local administration is by no means free from check and rein. Public opinion presses hard upon him, and " The People" to the mayor does not mean a little knot of party-workers, as it does to the alderman. The mayor's position makes him sensitive to the blame or approval of a wide and large constituency, the real people. The public opinion of the counting-house, the press, and the pulpit is the most terrible of critics, and the most inexorable of judges. The mere consciousness of this tribunal is often enough to strengthen the moral backbone of a weak man, and to elevate an average citizen into an ideal public officer. Executive officials, from mayor to President, are illustrations of this. Furthermore, the courts of law are always open, and the right of impeachment should be a recognized privilege and a vigorous possibility. The practical freedom from the judiciary which the executive enjoys is impolitic, and is the great defect in what may be called " The Brooklyn Idea " of city government. A bad mayor may do nothing which can bring him under the criminal jurisdiction of the courts. Public opinion is the hand that threatens him, but it may have no weapon with which to strike until the far-off election-day. Moreover, we are such fools that we make a fetich out of a party-name and abase ourselves before a shadow. Party-ties are so strong that, in Brooklyn's last city election, a very small change of votes would have defeated the admirable mayor, Low, and elected an unknown and untried competitor.[1]

ADMINISTRATIVE COURTS.

It is just that the appointing power should also possess the right to suspend or remove. If, however, the whole Execu-

---

[1] Written in the summer of 1885.

tive Department rests in the hand of the mayor, a bad mayor may do much to destroy the good that his predecessor created, and yet may not become liable to ordinary process of law. It seems to me that the continued success of a reformed municipal service may be more thoroughly assured by the introduction of administrative courts. These courts are well known in Europe, and there is nothing in their constitution or functions which is in any manner repugnant to our customs and institutions. Administrative courts exist for the examination and settlement of all official differences between members of the administration, and for adjudication between officers and the non-official world in disputes that affect administration solely. Complaints against public servants are brought before these courts, and a judicial inquiry is at once set on foot. Incompetent or untrustworthy officers are called to answer for their derelictions before the administrative court, and an adverse verdict is ground and sufficient motive for the culprit's dismissal.[1]

If powers like these could be conferred upon our city and county judiciaries, or, better still, upon a separate system of municipal administrative courts, with the right of appeal to the higher tribunals, and if, within proper limits, removals or interferences with the course of promotion could be based only upon the decisions of such courts, a long stride would have been taken toward a model municipal service. The proposed court, if judiciously constituted, would powerfully support a good government, or restrain a bad one. No objection could then be urged against the plan of appointments by the mayor. The tenure of office would sooner or later depend largely upon good behavior, and the idea might, at least, begin to penetrate the mind of the citizen that the

---

[1] In German cities a " Complaint-Book " (Beschwoerdebuch) is kept under the inspection of the authorities, and any one who discovers instances of official incapacity or injustice describes in that book his grievance. The complaints are examined and, if necessary, investigated by the officers of the administrative court, and the faults, if there be any, are punished.

mayoralty also is an office which demands a good administrator, and not a politician, and which, when once well filled, should retain its occupant as long as possible.

Frequent Elections.

There is already a tendency in the New Haven municipality toward lengthening terms of service. In the early history of the city a public officer remained at his post until death removed him. With the rise of the Jacksonian Democracy annual changes became more frequent. The reaction has been small and slow. In 1860, some daring spirits broached the idea that a two-years' term for the mayor would not endanger the popular liberties. That suggestion finally found favor, and now all the principal commissioners serve for three years. In town and city there are now in all forty-three officers who serve for three years. Perhaps the existing tendency may be carried still further without harm. If the mayor could have at least a three-years' term, and the subordinate members of the administration a much longer term, the city would profit by the increased experience and security of its servants. Professional politicians are the gainers by frequent elections.

The Board of Councilmen.

Why is it that, in city and nation alike, the Legislature incurs distrust? Why is it that in most of our cities the legislative branch contains so many men unfit for public trusts? The great majority of New Haven's councilmen undoubtedly desire to promote the city's best interests, but at the same time many of them are not men who can form an exalted idea of the city's best interests. If the Court of Common Council should lose its powers of patronage, of appointment, of political coercion, membership in it would be less inviting to the small politician, and more so to the better sort of citizen.

It is difficult to see what would be lost if the Board of Councilmen should be abolished, and if the City Council should consist of aldermen alone. There is and has been no respectable reason for the existence of the lower council, except the fact that it helped complete the analogy between the city, State, and National governments. The argument which Washington used to justify the division of the National Congress into two houses is adduced as a support for the bicameral council—viz.: the assurance of dignified and calm consideration. But undue haste in legislation may be prevented by requiring an interval between the proposal and the passage of an ordinance, and by publishing the proposition in the newspapers during that interval. It has been found, also, that if any potent interests demand hurried law-making, the mere existence of two branches in the council is a very small obstacle.

Moreover, there is no federative principle that seeks preservation in a city. Two chambers should imply two constituencies. A second chamber might explain its existence if it were chosen by a body of taxpayers. But the aldermen are as completely representative of the people and of the wards as the councilmen are. It is time that the complete distinction in essence between a corporate government and a nation should be admitted on all sides.

The fact that New Haven was once an isolated community with aspirations toward independence does not affect the consideration of the present city government and its needs. As Mr. Simon Sterne has clearly pointed out, the modern city is a corporation, charged with the administration of property, and, properly, so far as its internal operations are concerned, it has no political functions whatever. The administration of a city government should therefore be executed with ideas and methods similar to those which other corporations find advantageous. Nobody can say that the boards of aldermen and of councilmen contain very different material, either in respect to age or wisdom. The lower board is merely an additional house of refuge for the ambitious aspirant and the corner-grocery politician. No healthy corporation would retain in its service two organs when one could do all the allotted work as well.

Let the Board of Councilmen, therefore, be evolved out of existence. Then if, in addition to the aldermen from wards, there were chosen aldermen-at-large in numbers proportioned to population, perhaps one to every full ten thousand, allowance being made for minority representation, the New Haven Council would count to-day thirty-one members—a good working number for a city legislature.

The charter of the city wisely provides that the presidents of the various commissions in the city government shall be entitled to seats in either branch of the council, with every privilege except that of voting. It would be no more than an expansion of the same idea if all ex-mayors who had been elected by the people, and who had served honorably throughout their terms, should be entitled to membership in the Board of Aldermen. The honor might include the right to vote, and might cease in case of removal from the city or of election to another office. Most of the incumbents of the mayoralty attain that height after having served the city in less important trusts. That the city should lose the benefit of their ripest judgment and experience is faulty economy and poor politics. The reasons that support the retirement of ex-Presidents to the Senate for life also favor the theory that ex-mayors should continue to aid the city which has honored them. There are additional arguments in the case of the mayor. Membership in the Board of Aldermen would convey now no social distinction. It would be a continuation of public work rather than the bestowal of a public reward.

THE CHOICE OF ALDERMEN.

However, it seems to me that still better results could be attained by a still more radical change, by a change in the

mode of election.   In many quarters the opinion gains ground
that ward representation is corrupting and belittling, and
that aldermen ought to be elected on a general ticket by the
people at large.

New Haven has completed its first century of city-life, and
for only thirty-two years of that time have wards existed.
In the earlier day the best men in the city were honored by
the name of alderman.   It is not always so now.   The plea
that an alderman should be able to champion the "Local
interests" of a ward is a strong argument against electing
aldermen by wards.   What broad-minded and upright man
will care to sit in the City Council, knowing that he is
expected to secure as large a slice as possible of the public
funds for improvements in his locality—jobs which will
bring money into his ward and into the pockets of the clique
that worked for his nomination?   How can any but the
small-minded man set himself to represent or to uphold the
alleged "Interests" of a few square feet of ground?[1]

---

[1] That species of city councilman whose highest idea of achievement for
the public good is to keep his band of local workers "solid," to assist the
more importunate of them to jobs at repaving streets—in his own ward, if
possible—and to vote taxes that better men must pay, has become an
object so familiar as to be almost unnoticed.

An exceptionally fine specimen of the performances of these Solons is
preserved in Baltimore, a city whose municipal government is deplorably
bad.   During Mayor Latrobe's first administration, a certain district was
represented in the City Council by a nonentity whose only claim to political
preferment was his affiliation with the controlling clique.   This councilman, being unable to secure a sewer, or freshly painted street-signs for his
district, cast about him for some other means of vindicating his fitness for
public trust and his reputation of watchfulness for the needs of his locality.
One day the political magnates of the neighborhood were holding sweet
converse in their customary headquarters, the corner grocery.   A bright
idea flashed upon the intellect of the councilman.   He observed that every
district in the city except his own had an avenue.   Such injustice should
be redressed, and he solemnly consecrated himself, amid the plaudits of his
comrades, to the work of securing an avenue for his suffering district.

The party decided that Choptank street, which extends across the district, should be the future avenue; but with what name should it be

The ward-workers of either party can nominate a mediocre man for aldermanic honors, confident that their neighbors will not bolt the ticket, because their man is the regular nominee, even if there is no worse reason. The rest of the city knows very little about the ward or its candidates, and can have no voice in their election, at any rate ; and so the ward elects a bad alderman. If, on the other hand, the city convention which nominates a mayor should, in a similar way, nominate aldermen, there would be a better chance of securing aldermen whose mental and moral calibre would be as good as that of the mayor. If the whole city were to be the constituency of each alderman, the candidates would be more closely scrutinized by both the press and the people. The best citizens would be more likely to desire aldermanic honor if it were the gift of the whole community, and not of a comparatively insignificant group in that community.

The root of the whole matter is in the primaries. Unless

---

christened ? Some member of the company, with more intelligence than the rest, waggishly and maliciously proposed that Choptank street should become Collington avenue, in honor of the renowned English admiral, Lord Collington. Seeing that the proposal was favorably received, he narrated the services and many exploits of Lord Collington, who had, forsooth, crowned a long and illustrious career by commanding the fleet which brought to Maryland its first settlers at St. Mary's. Yet this noble mariner's name was not preserved in a single street or alley of the whole city of Baltimore. The story was greedily swallowed, and the councilman was unanimously advised to rescue Admiral Collington from the oblivion into which he had undeservedly fallen. In due time a bill was offered in the Board of Councilmen changing Choptank street—in its course through that district only—to Collington avenue, and the wondrous history of the name was recited.

Playing with the names of streets is recognized as a prerogative of Baltimore councilmen, and such bills pass as if by an act of personal courtesy. There is nothing to show that bill and story were objected to in either branch of the City Council. But in the mayor's office there was some one who knew a little history.

Mayor Latrobe sent to the council a message exposing the absurdity of the Collington anecdote, and berating the honorable gentlemen for their disregard of everybody's convenience excepting their own, *but His Honor signed the bill.*

the better elements in each party attend and control the primaries, reform-movements will always limp. To elect a good mayor and leave the City Council and the primaries in their present status is only to whitewash the same old sepulchre.[1] If aldermen are chosen by wards, the primaries determine who the candidates shall be. If the aldermen are chosen upon a general ticket, the primaries can elect only delegates to the nominating convention. It must be that the latter distribution of powers is incomparably the safer.

The first and last need of New Haven's government is one which it shares in common with all institutions—the need of intelligent and conscientious discussion. Children in the schools should be familiarized with the working of the different governments under which they live; but that instruction is only a small part of the requisite political education.

The press, the bar, the pulpit, and the private citizen should actively teach and preach upon the subject, and disseminate the doctrines that local taxation furnishes problems as pressing as those of the national tariff; that a high standard of morality is as essential for the City Hall as for the Church; and that the choice of clear-headed and honest men of business for municipal offices is as vital a matter as the election of Democrat or Republican to the Presidency. Then, perchance, one might obtain a little clearer vision of that better age of municipal government to which the gliding years are leading us, wherein the local machinery shall move almost unaffected by political influences and revolutions; wherein men grow gray in faithful public service without fear of removal; wherein the right of municipal suffrage is

---

[1] A recent writer has suggested that one way to improve primaries is to improve the surroundings of primaries. They are too often held in or near some low groggery—in rooms where the more decent citizens would dislike to go. Of course, this does not excuse the decent citizen, who ought to go, and to help secure for his party a more respectable cradle. A city ordinance might compel every ward or district to provide a ward-hall free to all parties, suitable for public meetings, remote from saloons—a place where every voter might be glad to go.

proportioned to the burden of taxation that is borne;[1] and
wherein every organ and every officer of the municipality
feels an actual responsibility not only to superior organs and
officers and to the people, but, more immediately, to the
courts of the community; "To the end," as the old Puritans
phrased it, "it may be a government of lawes and not of
men."

---

[1] Is this doctrine thought undemocratic? There can be no better Democratic authority than the following : " Municipal officers, having no power
over persons, but only that of applying the proceeds of taxes, ought to
be elected by those alone who contribute to such payments."—*Albert
Gallatin* (1833).

www.ingramcontent.com/pod-product-compliance
Lightning Source LLC
Chambersburg PA
CBHW032157010726
47493CB00008BA/2726